Life **d**

A novel by

J.D. Hollyfield

Cover Design: Yocla Designs
www.yocladesigns.com

Edited by: Michelle Josette
www.mjbookeditor.com

To Jeff. Thank you for being so awesome.

Life in a Rut, Love not Included
A novel by
J.D. Hollyfield

Table of Contents

Chapter 1

Waking up is hard to do... Or wait, is it waking up or breaking up? Either way, I get to do both.

I am at the best part of the most amazing dream of my life. This hot brute of a dream man is working his way up my body, tasting every part of me. I can practically feel myself squirming in my sleep. His hot tongue brushing against my naval is going to make me wake up screaming. My dream man takes his strong hands and works his way up my stomach to grab at my breasts and squeeze. His head dips to my breast and I can feel his breath over my nipple. *Oh god! This is about to get good.* He works his magic on B #1 then transports his sexy mouth to B #2. I arch my back to give him better access. I'm pretty sure if someone is watching me sleep right now, they'll think I'm having an exorcism.

After his dirty assault on my breasts, he lifts his head and slithers his way up my body. I can feel his gigantic hard self on my belly. Holy rock of a man, he is hard everywhere! The thought that I am about to have some mind-tingling hot and sweaty dream sex is going to send me into oblivion. My brute lover lowers his head and presses his mouth to my neck. I hear him speak my name as he works his way to my earlobe with his lips. *Oh god!* He is sucking on my earlobe. I love that mouth of his... "Sarah," he whispers, and bites sensually on my shoulder. This may be better than any foreplay I have experienced in real life, and I am soon about to explode.

"Sarah..." There it is again. My name.

I hear him repeat my name but unfortunately this fantasy is soon becoming a nightmare as I swear his voice is sounding more like my mother's.

Focus, Sarah. I attempt to cling onto whatever his name is – no need to exchange real names, as this is in fact only my dream.

"Sarah…" There it is again!

Ignore! Ignore! Ignore!

"Stay focused," my inner voice whispers to me. It's about time I get this moving along, because I have a feeling things are about to get real, real fast. I wrap my legs around my hunky dream man and attempt to guide him toward my warm spot. I feel his strong arms wrap around me. His soft breath hits my ear, and just as he is about to push home, he whispers, "It's not you—"

"SARAH! Get up, you're going to be late to pick up Aunt Raines!"

And Bam!

Reality.

My life.

Once again, I awake to a pitiful reality. My name is Sarah Sullivan and I am stuck in a rut, and it's called my life. I am thirty-one years old and I have a feeling at some point in my life I may have taken a wrong turn. I can't even seem to have a dream without it interacting with reality and ruining what "could have been".

I haven't always been this pathetic. Up until three months ago, I had a boyfriend, a best friend, a killer job and a beautiful life. I had *purpose*. I had things...figured out. Or at least I thought I did. I guess I was what you would call a victim of being blind to the world outside her perfect little bubble. It's scary how easy it is to get so wrapped up in your own bubble of life that you fail to see what's really going wrong on the outside. Sad to say, apparently everything was going wrong outside of mine.

I mean, geez, where should I start?

Well, I guess we'll get the most hated out of the way first: the ex-boyfriend. The one and only Mr. Steve Hamilton. Precious Steve Hamilton, Vice President of Marketing— also known as the son of the President/Owner—at Hamilton Corp, the most prestigious advertising agency in Chicago. I would like to refer to him henceforth as the Golden Jerk.

Okay, now that we have his title defined, let's take a walk down memory lane and see how the Golden Jerk took part in popping my little bubble.

The beginning of the end started seven years ago when my life actually caught that "lucky break" people talk about. Everyone wishes for the day when they finally have everything they've ever wished for, and gladly pat themselves on the back for making it happen. Well, that was me. At twenty-four, and semi fresh out of college, I not only landed a killer advertising job in Chicago, I also landed the gorgeous son of the President of said advertising firm.

Insert Steve Hamilton.

Steve was everything a girl dreamed of. He was tall—an impressive six-foot-two—with broad shoulders, silky blonde hair and to-die-for eyes. I can still picture myself staring into those golden-brown eyes, thinking I was the luckiest girl alive. *Gag...*

Okay, moving on.

Working closely together on projects, Steve and I hit it off in no time. It didn't take long for him to pursue me and for me to give in, more than willingly. We were dating in a matter of weeks from our first meeting. There was no better feeling than when Steve would put his arms around me and nibble at the baseline of my neck, whisper how much he adored the touch of my skin and how much he loved me. Our personal lives were the same. I had a great apartment with my roommate and best friend, Stacey, and he had an insanely expensive condo in the ritziest neighborhood in downtown Chicago. As it goes, each place had held each other's toothbrushes, our clothes filled each other's drawers, and frames scattered around filled with the happiest times of our life together. We were in love. We even got to work together and spend crazy amounts of time with one another and luckily enough, even combine our friend groups. I had a great best friend, which meant now, so did he. Life was perfect.

Yeah, of course, after a while things did slow down a little. But whose relationship doesn't? Years passed and things grew calm. Steve got a bit more controlling, sure, but who wouldn't in his position? Being at the top of a company, it was important that he kept appearances. His assertiveness and demands on my looks were always a must. Letting Steve down in a public setting was never an option. If one did not perform, Steve made sure there were consequences. It was hard at times being the girlfriend of the man on top. But no one is perfect. I was still crazy in love with Steve and was always hoping in the back of my mind that one day he would ask me those four special words every girl waits to hear... But he never did and I was patient so I continued on with life as usual, maintaining the status quo.

Our routine.

Before I get too far ahead of myself though, let's introduce the second most hated person on my list.

Insert former roommate, former best friend, Stacey Gibbs.

After college, I was in deep search of a roommate. Luck had it that after an extensive search on Craigslist, I found Stacey. Turns out we were a friendship match made in heaven. In no time, we were bunking in a gorgeous apartment together, embarking on a new Best Friend's Forever life. Now, if you thought Steve and I sounded inseparable, then double that with Stacey and me. We had to have been separated at birth. Not that we looked anything alike. Stacey wore the perfect shade of shoulder-length blonde hair, with model thin legs and a killer body, and perfect peaches-and-cream skin that illumined her natural tones. She didn't have to wear makeup to have men drop dead over her, but she loved makeup so anything she did made her look even more flawless.

Stacey also came from money and had that rich blood in her. No worries for me, because she was a sharer and she wanted her best friend to also indulge in the finer things. Money was never an issue as long as we were together. Enter stage left: my new wardrobes and new appreciation for silk and the word Prada. We were two girls having the time of our lives, with youth and beauty and money to boot.

Things couldn't have been better. I had to admit that if someone asked me about those years of my life, I would have been able to say that I had everything I had ever wanted. Steve loved me, and I loved him. I had Stacey, the sister I'd always wanted, and I was quickly working my way up the ladder at Hamilton Corp. I was living out my dream of being successful, in love and happy. I looked good, I felt good, and I even had that blissful little skip to my step.

That skip turned into a fumble and then a smack and a pop to my perfect bubble, when my happy little life came to a screeching halt. They don't lie when they say that your life can change in the blink of an eye. Because literally I blinked, and my life was gone. All's it took was me coming home early one day to my perfect swanky apartment to find my perfect boyfriend and my perfect best friend in my perfect bed together. I don't think I have to go too much into what happens next. Pretty much delete the perfect boyfriend, perfect friend, perfect apartment and later, perfect job out of my equation and add three months of solitude, and here I am.

It has been three months since my bubble exploded, and I mean like with a Boom! Bam! POW!

As in a *SPLAT!* In my face. If you look closely enough, I think I still might have pieces of bubble stuck to my skin... Or my pride, either way. I had to crawl home to my parents, who definitely did not see this coming since they turned my room into one of those storage rooms where Home Shopping Network junk goes to die.

So, to sum up, I am boyfriend-less, jobless, friendless and lifeless. And if we're being honest here, you can add depression to that long list as well.

"SARAH! This is the last time I am going to call your name, then I am sending your father in there to revive you!"

Oh great, not Dad. Have you ever been fully woken up by a retired Navy commander? I brace my ears with a pillow wrapped around the back of my head.

"I'm up, geez, call off the guards!" I moan. It's not like I can sit here and stare at my ceiling much longer anyway. My dream man has faded into the abyss of my subconscious, and he was probably about to break up with me anyway. Go figure. I throw my legs off my bed and begin my descent to stand. "Today is going to be a better day," I tell myself. "Today I will shower. I will brush my hair. I will do something positive… "

Humph!

Apparently I am too busy with my "Go get 'em" speech to realize I have my sheet wrapped around my leg and so I end my lecture with a face full of carpet.

Yep, this is my life.

I officially take my speech back.

I start to crawl back into bed, since that's obviously where I should have stayed to begin with. Of course, I miss my calling, as my door flies open. And here pops in dear old Dad.

"Soldier! You heard your mother! Now, your Aunt Raines is waiting promptly at the airport at eleven hundred hours.

You will obey your mother and complete this task. Living here is not your free ride..."

"Ugh. I'm up, Dad. Thanks for reminding me of my life success," I groan.

Apparently he is not done. "I raised you to be a strong individual, Sarah. I worked for this country so you can have a fair life and a strong education. I did not raise you to be thrown around by a man of no dignity and have you run back home to hide," he continues, standing firmly in my doorway. "And again, I am still waiting on the explanation of why you decided to quit a very lucrative position at that firm. I didn't raise you to back down, especially because of a man. Use your brain, not your heart. How many times—"

"THANK YOU, Dad! I'm up and this is only going to delay me picking up Aunt Raines!" I not so sweetly belt out while pushing him out of my door gently but in a thirteen-year-old get-out-of-my-room sort of way. I'm thirty-one and living at home being lectured by my parents, so I might as well act like a thirteen-year-old.

Having to explain to my parents that I was dumped by my high-profile boyfriend was one thing. Having to tell them I quit my job abruptly was another. I think it was the "I need to move back home just until I get myself back on my feet" speech that really threw them. I had been like any striving teenager right out of high school. I wanted out. I went to college practically running, because it meant getting out of my parents' house and reach. I was a suffocating "young adult" who needed to live on her own and experience life and create a resume for herself so she could use those credentials to define her ambitions and be huge!

I graduated from the University of Illinois with a 3.9 GPA in Marketing and a hefty hangover. Then again, what was college for, if not to experience boys and binges? I worked nights at a popular bar and saved my money, knowing the second I stepped foot off that campus I was going to start my life. On my own. And I was definitely, most certainly, not going back home.

I set up roommate wanted ads on the Internet before I left school since let's be honest, I was a bartender, not a pole dancer, so living the life I wanted on my own was a little higher up from where I was on my accomplishment list. But it only took four scary interviews—one who didn't even speak English, which I actually debated wouldn't be such a bad thing—before I found Stacey, a.k.a. Boyfriend Stealer. The Stacey who turned out to be a huge game-changer in my life.

As I mentioned earlier, Stacey had come from a wealthy family of high-bred heritage. She was an only child and, like me, she shared the urge to run fast out of her parents' home and live on her own. As her family wanted her to commute from home, she chose to take her chances and find a place on her own. Stacey was originally from New York; her family moved to Chicago since her father was opening up a new branch of family banks. The life of the rich I guess. When Stacey saw my ad on Craigslist she also admitted to friendship love at first sight. We had clicked immediately and talked for hours before moving in together so it felt like we had known each other for years by the time we actually took the plunge. We found a swanky apartment on the Upper North Side of Chicago, just big enough to fit all of our stuff (well, *her* stuff, since her family insisted she own the best appliances, furniture and electronics possible). I would have had to sell all my organs to afford a week's worth of rent at our place, but what Stacey wanted, Stacey got. Really.

The apartment was something out of a magazine. Our furniture was all top of the line. Stacey was obsessed with purple so of course she convinced me that the purple velvet set would look fantastic. It was also her money and if she wanted to spend $7,000 on sofas then I wasn't going to stop her. We had a spacious kitchen that was, again, top of the line. Not sure why we needed two ovens, since I'm pretty sure Stacey had never cooked a meal in her life, but I loved it since I came from a homely background and cooking was a hobby I'd always enjoyed. Skimming over the obviously gigantic flat screen TVs and the expensive framed artwork that hung on the walls, we also both had our own master bed and bath. As a perk of being Stacey Gibbs' roommate and new best friend, I received a four-poster king size bed, which she insisted I complement with a purple and gray down comforter duvet. She herself had a similar setup; Stacey insisted that everything match.

Both suites came with a wall of ceiling-to-floor windows looking out on a stunning view of downtown Chicago. At night, the lights from the skyscrapers would illuminate my bedroom. Everything in the apartment was covered in Persian tile or marble. My bathroom itself was draped from counter to shower with pure luxury. I remember thinking if times ever got tough I would just start chipping away at my bathroom sink for cash.

It was surreal. I was twenty-four years old and on my own. It felt like a breath of fresh air—even fresher since it wasn't a college campus and the smell of puke didn't permanently linger no matter how hard you scrubbed.

Who would have thought that I would be living on my own, in one of the greatest cities in the world?!

I won't lie, at first I was a bit worried about the financial differences between us. Now, I was not raised from money. Having a naval commander as a father, I was taught strict rules about how far a dollar could be stretched. Living with Stacey, it was a bit unnerving to see her blow money like it was water. Well maybe not water. That's not so free nowadays either. Let's just say she liked to spend, and she liked to share.

Suddenly it seemed that everything in my life had started to change. I exchanged my Converse sneakers for Gucci heals and my hoodies for Fendi wrap-around blouses. Now that I look back, it's sad how easily I let someone—or rather, two people—change me into someone else. You would never have known where I came from, who I once was, by the way I had been molded into the person I had slowly become.

Chapter 2

I peek out my bedroom door to make sure it is safe to venture into the hallway, and head towards the bathroom. After taking a whiff of myself and realizing life's not all it's cracked up to be, I decide to scratch showering off my list of goals for the day and just stick to the basics, which come in the form of toothpaste and a stick of deodorant. I haven't bothered unpacking my fancy things that came along with The Stacey Roommate Plan, like my electric toothbrush, so at the moment I am currently using a 1980s normal non-vibrating toothbrush while gagging on my parents' original, probably first addition ever, Crest toothpaste.

I have yet to take the plunge and unpack my stuff. I figure, why bother? I don't plan on going anywhere anytime soon anyway.

Now let me be the first one to tell you that wallowing in one's self-pity is a full time job. It has a tendency to take away from the other semi more important things in one's life, such as hygiene and self-awareness. One major step I have been avoiding during my "poor me" parade is looking in the mirror. I have spent so much time self-loathing and crying like a baby that I am not too sure I want to take a look at the loser I have become. The only good thing that came out of this is the weight loss, which we can thank not eating for, due to my pitiful life blowing up in my face. (Please refer back to bubble splatter.) I figure since I knocked off showering, I do have an opening in my appointment booked to look up and judge.

I am staring into the eyes of a stranger. *Well...I can probably do without the bags under my eyes*, I think while I try to calculate when the last time was that I had an eyebrow wax or a proper hair dye. Some things, whether your life is ending or not, should just not be neglected. *I look awesome...for a homeless person.* "Well that's enough for today," I say to no one in particular, then I spit, rinse, and turn to "complete my task" for the day.

Behind all the fancy clothes and designer toothbrushes, I was no one special to begin with. Standing at an unimpressive height of 5'4", I have normal brown hair, sometimes referred to as my "mop", and fair skin since I'm no longer following Stacey's daily ritual of self-tanner. I had eyes the shade of the sea, per Steve. Now they are just hazel-ish green. Who gives such lame compliments and falls for them anyway? Ugh. Shades of the sea. Vomit.

I've always had a great metabolism so weight was never really an issue, but Stacey insisted we attend classes together at the gym. If it wasn't to look fit, it was to meet guys. No complaints about a little sweat if a pack of tanned abs came along with it.

With Stacey being the stereotypical tall, beautiful blonde, I'm not sure anyone would have acknowledged my presence if it wasn't for my incredible rack. I know. How self-righteous am I? But a girl can't lie. If she's got the goods, she knows it. In the end my rack didn't keep the guy so who cares anyway?

Onward toward my day in Loserville.

My parents live in a small ranch house in Oak Park, Illinois, just outside of Chicago. They bought it once my dad was finally able to settle down after the Navy and they never left. It's a three bedroom split-level ranch house that makes you feel like you ventured back into the 70s every time you walk in. Ah, the life. I really hope their decorating skills rub off on me. Not.

I always hated the suburbs. I hated the cattiness of all the neighborhood kids. Did you fit in? Were you the bully or the geek? I hated that if you didn't swagger along with the other kids on the street you would get bullied to not be allowed to use their side of the sidewalk. Petty little kids. Add it to the list of things to do today: finally use the sidewalk. I'm thirty-one. No one's going to tell me what to do anymore.

Walking into the kitchen, I spot my mother at the stove doing what she does best: cook. Surprisingly enough, no one in our family is overweight due to her extreme expertise on how to make a gourmet meal. It is beyond me. Well, I take that back. Looking at my dad at the table in his overalls, he is looking a bit snug.

"Well finally, dear, it took you long enough. Are you hungry? I have a list of things I need you to do today. Feel free to take your aunt with you or drop her off first," my sweet mother recites. Nothing like being bossed around, but in a sweet motherly way.

"No thanks, I already ate," I reply, regarding her breakfast invitation, thinking about the extra toothpaste I indulged in earlier. "So, what kind of 'things' are you requesting here?" I ask suspiciously. Seriously, if my mother sends me to her hairdresser's house again, just so she can attempt to hook me up with her forty-year-old live-in son, I'm going to vomit.

"Well, your father and I have been talking about building an addition to the back of the house, and I need you to go pick up the blueprints from our contractor. It's not far out of your way."

"Do I get gas money out of this?" I ask.

"Do we get rent money out of you?" my father chimes in.

"Fair enough." Ugh, I hate when I lose.

"Speaking of which," Dad continues, "when are you going to start looking for a job? You are wasting away that education I paid for."

"Oh Harold, leave her alone. She is doing the best she can, aren't you dear?" *Go mom!*

"I have some potential companies in mind. I am buttering up my resume and am going to scope them out sometime this week." Lie.

"Which ones?" my dad asks.

"There is this really big marketing firm in the city." Lie. Lie. "They are interested in my background." Lie. Lie. Lie. "I will be in touch with them later this week." My nose is growing so long, it is literally spelling out the word *lie*.

"Well that's great dear!" my mom praises. "Keep us posted. We are rooting for you." Will do!

I don't know why it is so important for everyone to have a job. A job doesn't make a person. Mr. Henderson's son, Hank, doesn't have a job and he seems fine. But he was also in jail for a while and is now living off government money so, whatever. Money is money, right? Is being dumped considered a disability? Note to self: check into government payouts.

If I was honest with myself I would say that I haven't spent an ounce of my free will looking for a new job. The truth is I really am afraid. I worked at Hamilton Corp for almost seven years before I openly expressed my not-so-pleasant feelings for Steve in front of the whole management board, then quit. How am I supposed to go into an interview with my one and only job as a reference? "We were going to hire you until we cross-checked your reference and they told us what a freak show you are. Thanks anyways!"

Do I regret what I did? Maybe. A little. Well yes. Who wouldn't? I busted my nice little ass at that job and spent seven years crawling my way to the position I was in, only to have it ruined by some asshat. And I remember being so excited when I got that damn job.

Insert Hamilton Corp.

I had been searching for a job for what felt like eons, but I never got a call back or any acceptance letters. I didn't get to the point of panic since Stacey's parents were practically paying for our rent in full at this point and I still had a comfortable savings to live off of.

Then one day I landed an interview for Hamilton Corp. It was huge. I had been sick all morning with nerves, worried I was going to blow it and end up barfing on myself mid-interview. I had arrived there early and practiced all my questions and answers over and over again. I had my portfolio with me, primped and ready to shine. I sat and waited to be called in. And I waited...and waited some more. Finally, when I asked the secretary what the deal was, she replied that the position had been filled an hour ago and they were not taking any more candidates. Before I could strangle her or cry like a baby—I couldn't tell which I wanted to do more—I told her to have a nice day, while in my head I said other things, and hurriedly left through the gigantic glass doors I'd come in through.

While scurrying through the lobby, I decided it was a good time to turn on my waterworks and did a bee-line for the bathroom. While in mid-turn I not so ladylike body-slammed into a hard male figure, knocking all of the papers out of his hand and watched them scatter all over the marble lobby floor. Horrified to say the least, I apologized to this guy, or god, whatever you want to call someone standing at an impressive six-foot-two, golden eyes and a body that screams, "Lick me all over." Then Mr. Lick-me-all-over kindly helped me steady my legs while asking if I was OK. I had helped him pick up his papers and apologized again. He didn't take no for an answer, and convinced me to join him for coffee and discuss why I was upset. Turns out Mr. Lick-me-all-over was the son of Hamilton Corp and the job—my job—was handed straight to him due to his bloodline, no interview required. He had introduced himself as Steve, and insisted he help "squeeze me in" since he had rudely stolen my job.

We talked and laughed as the hours passed. He had put in a few calls, me insisting he not, since it was embarrassing enough, and before you knew it I was working as an intern for Hamilton Corp. I know. Intern. It was not paid, but it was something. It was the best he could do, since he said they weren't actually hiring at all. I would take it. It took me three months to get hired on full time, and before I knew it, I was working my way to becoming *the* marketing specialist for their top ten clients.

Seven years later and another notch on the unemployment list, here I am. No more fancy job title. No more fancy boyfriend.

Insert present: Living with my parents. Oh god, I think I'm going to be sick.

Chapter 3

Venturing out of the house is always tricky. As I said before, I haven't really done much unpacking. I guess it's because I am still in a bit of denial of my present living situation, or life situation at that. I kind of still believe that this is all just a bad dream and I'm going to wake up soon, and why spend half my dream unpacking? I have lived in the same shirt and sweats for most of the time I've been home and only peal them off of me so I can shower (which is not often) and my mother steals them to clean so I can put them back on. Taking my pathetic self out into the world requires a bit more attire.

I stumble to the garage and grab the first box I see. Whatever is in it, I will put on. If it's a lampshade, then it's on. I don't care. My mother convinced me to go grocery shopping for her last week, hoping to get me out of the house. Of course I simply put my shoes on and went. Apparently people in this town still judge and gossip, because before I was done I got a call from my poor mother asking me to just head home. Gotta love the suburbs.

First box contains my shoes. My loves. If there is anything I stand true to, it is my love for shoes. I would save full paychecks just to buy myself a beautiful pair of Jimmy Choos, or with an extra big check, Louboutins. They were just so enticing. Addicting. Obsessive.

OK, I have more shoes than clothes, but at least I earned them. I worked for the money, baby. So I pull out a pair of my nice shiny gold stiletto-healed Manolo Blahniks. I still remember when I bought them. I had locked down one of my first clients: the clothing line for Macy's Brand. Add a hefty bonus, and insert shoe purchase. The second I paid for them I slipped them on my feet and they fit like a glove. I think I wore them for a week straight, whether they matched my outfit or not. I remember Stacey, Steve and I went dancing to one of the new nightclubs in the city and I danced all night in them. Steve ended up having to carry me home since my feet we so blistered. Stupid Steve. "Don't worry, Manolos," I said to myself. "I won't let Steve ruin our friendship." I take out my shoes and stick to my guns. First box. A deal's a deal.

After getting ready (or whatever you call what it is I look like), I venture downstairs. I see the note and list Mom left me on the table. Reading the note, it seems Mom and Dad ditched me to go to the neighbors' for tea time. How lovely.

Old people. I never want to be one.

I grab my purse, car keys, list, and directions and head out to my parents' 1980 station wagon. Let's be honest, who needs a car in the city? I didn't. I walked or took the sub, or had Steve or Stacey's drivers take me everywhere. Also, who needs a new shiny one? Apparently not my parents.

Reading my mother's note again, only because I can't read chicken scrabble that well on the first round, I attempt to locate the address she gave me on my phone to pick up these blueprints. I figure if I can scoop those up first, then make it in time to pick up Aunt Raines, I will have a smooth morning and be back in bed before noon. I know one thing is for certain and that is that I am definitely not going to miss the Golden Girls marathon.

I head east onto Waverly Avenue to start my quest. I make it out of the neighborhood and onto the main road and see an abundance of red break lights. What I did not expect was traffic. Ugh. Who is even on the streets at this time? Aren't people supposed to be at work? See, that's what's wrong with society today. Nobody is working. Too busy clogging up the streets so no one can get to where they are going. Staring at the time tick away, I pretty much start to sweat at the bad choices I have just recently made. Not that Aunt Raines will mind waiting, but my Naval commander dad will have my ass if I fail at this task. Time to think, Sarah. Think!

It's been a while since I lived around here and trying to remember what is where is a bit tricky. I look at the GPS on my phone in an attempt to find an alternate route, just as the car behind me starts honking.

"Geez, relax pal!" I yell out my window as I accelerate. Multitasking was one of the major bullet points on my resume, as well as my job title. Apparently trying to drive, GPS it, *and* yell at the guy behind me does not qualify as a positive multitasking ability, as it takes me three seconds of doing so to ram into the guy in front of me.

Now...who the *HELL* honks at someone to move when it is not time to move?! *Great!* "Great!" This cannot be happening. Apparently the guy in front of me is thinking the same thing. He throws his hands in the air – not a good sign. This is so not good for my layout of time. I am definitely going to miss the first episode of the Girls.

Not sure really what to do—besides get out of the car and bash the guy behind me face-in—I start to look in the glove compartment for my parents' insurance. Because that's what you do, right? You hit someone, you exchange info and that's that. You both go on your merry way. I can do this. Except, I can't find any forms. *Seriously?* "Seriously!?" This day is NOT panning out for me. Note to self: stop taking demands from the parental units.

I watch the guy in front of me get out of his vehicle, and I assume I should do the same and slowly exit the 80s wagon. I can do this. Put on my sweet face. Apologize to fellow neighbor... "Are you fucking kidding me?!" he yells. *Whoa.* Did not see that one coming. "Don't you know how to drive, lady?!" Um...yes and no. "Can't you wait to text your damn boyfriend till you're not driving a vehicle?!" *If* I had a boyfriend, but he dumped me.

"I'm really sorry," I tell him. "I was trying to look at directions, and then the douche behind me honked, so I—"

Rude guy cuts me off again. "I'm running late for a meeting with a client, and now this!" He stops and stares at the damage done to his truck by the time machine wagon. If you would have asked me, I would have said it was no big deal, considering all the damage was done to the bumper. I mean, aren't those things made of rubber?

"I bet looking at this piece of shit you don't even have insurance, do you?!" OK, hold up, Hottie McAngry Pants. I mean, this guy is getting way too overheated. As we both turn from looking at the damage to each other, I notice how manly Hottie McAngry Pants actually is. At an impressive anger level of 8.5, he stands about 6'2", with strong facial features, dark hair and broad shoulders that I am actually daydreaming about putting my legs around. "Hello!? Are you even in there?!"

"Oh, yeah, sorry," I stutter. "Yes, for one I do have insurance. I'm sorry but this is my parents' car, so I'm not sure where it is. Can't we just trade information and I'll call you, or you call me and our insurance can work it out?" I stand there waiting for his answer, thinking it's not going to be what I want to hear, considering he looks like he just went up to a 9.5 on the anger scale.

"No sweetheart, we cannot just trade info. That's not how it works!" OK, let's step back for a second. As much as I would love for Hottie McAngry Pants to call me sweet nothings, it's not going to be rudely, in the middle of an intersection, while precious time is ticking away.

"Excuse me, mister. Like I said, this was an accident. It's not like I killed your family dog or anything so why don't you relax and it will get worked out. I'm sure my parents—" I am abruptly cut off when Hottie McAngry Pants takes that opportunity to snatch my phone right out of my non-manicured hands (which may I say need very badly), and tosses it into the intersection! I repeat! He tosses my phone! I watch it go flying, land splat in the road then get hit by about three vehicles before I turn to him open-mouthed. "You did not just do that." I breathe in a *holy shit I'm about to lose my cool* and match him on the angry scale.

"Learn to know when to use your phone! I'm taking your license," he says and takes his phone to snap a picture of my license plate, then he snatches my license out of my hand. "Don't worry, you will definitely hear from me!" He turns and starts to walk back to his truck.

As I stand there stunned, the only thing I can do is slowly repeat, "You did not just do that!" while Hottie McAngry

Pants climbs up in his truck, flips me the bird, and takes off.

That did *NOT* just happen! What is wrong with the world today? I mean, what kind of world do we live in when extremely hot guys, with tanned skin and rugged jaw lines, get all macho jerk on innocent people? I mean, seriously!

Honk! Honk!

"Oh shut up! I'm moving!" I yell at that car behind me. People just don't know how to go around. I get back into the retro wagon, and proceed onward a bit confused. Was that just a glitch in my ongoing bad dream or did that attractive douche just steal my license, hijack my phone only to murder it by a Saturn, and take off?! I should call the cops! *Yeah, with what phone?*

The even bigger issue now is that I have no idea where I am going and Aunt Raines is definitely going to have some waiting time. Great. I decide to skip the trip to the contractor and head first to the airport. It's safer to make the contractor wait than to have my dad kill me for my tardiness.

Pulling up to the airport I spot Aunt Raines immediately, sporting her gigantic tropical hat and piles of bags and jewelry dangling from her ears and neck and wrist. She is the all-American senior citizen. Retiring early to Florida years ago after Uncle Merle passed, Aunt Raines realized that she was missing out on so much, went nuts and decided to open up her own handmade jewelry store on the beach. I have mad respect for Aunt Raines, but her taste in jewelry is a bit out of my style. And when I say a bit, I mean huge. Like far. She spots the red box immediately and waves back. I slow to the curb.

"Hey, Auntie Raines! Sorry I'm late. I hit a little bump in the road." A.k.a. a nice piece of ass. *Like literally: ass,* I mumble to myself.

"No worries, sweet thang. You're here now. Let's get going though. I need to catch happy hour before dinner." Of course Aunt Raines always needed her happy dose of vermouth. Her ritual. She says it helps her not miss Uncle Merle so much. No biggie on my part. Any reason to indulge in a cocktail is good enough for me.

Since Aunt Raines doesn't own a phone, I have to stop at a payphone and call my mom for her contractor's address again. Who would have thought, payphones still do exist!

"Where are you, Sarah?" my mother belts through the phone. And when I say *belts*, I mean since I don't dare put the receiver too close to my ear without catching chlamydia (they may still exist but let's be honest, only hookers and drug dealers use payphones nowadays), I can still hear her. "You never showed at the contractors? He has called twice saying you were a no-show. He did not sound happy!"

"I understand," I tell her calmly. "I got into a little fender bender with the car. Everything's fine though. The guy was real nice about it. He's gonna call. Work it all out."

Lie.

"Well hurry up," she says. "Tell my sister I said hello and I have her vermouth waiting." Will do! After mentally writing down the address and swearing to my mother that

I know where I'm going—partial lie—Aunt Raines and I head together to our next destination.

As far as I know I am in the right place. I have to be since this is now the third place we have stopped and I have struck out every time. I mean, what kind of address is this? And who doesn't mark street signs? Once we make it down the gravel road, signs of life start to appear and I finally see a construction site with a huge trailer and a sign for Calloway Construction. Last goal. Get in and get out, vermouth and Golden Girls in T-minus twenty minutes. Mission complete.

"Hurry now, sweet thang. It's gettin' close to happy hour."

"I know Auntie, in and out. Sit tight," I chirp as I pull into a parking spot I believe I just made, then hop out.

As I make my way towards the trailer, I spot some men walking with tools and wood boards. I peak over, noticing all tan and muscle. Not bad, not bad. Why did I never date a construction worker? "Can I help you?" one of the men asks while walking closer to me.

"Um, yes. Thanks. I'm looking for Jack Calloway?"

"Is he expecting you?"

Man, tight ship they run around here. "Um, yeah, I'm supposed to be picking up some blueprints. He is doing work on my parents' house," I say while he and his buddies check me out.

As Mr. Tan-and-Wide finishes looking me up and down, he points to my left. "He's in his office. Second trailer to the left."

"Thanks!" I say, then turn toward my destination.

"No problem," he says to my back, then adds, "Nice shoes." When I turn around to look at Tan-and-Wide I catch him and his wingman smiling at me. I give him a courtesy wink and continue walking on. I can respect a man's appreciation for a good pair of shoes.

I walk up to the trailer and debate whether or not I need to knock. Deciding that it would take time off my end goal, I decide to just walk in. Time is of the essence, as they say. I open the door and step inside, looking around. "Hello?" I call out in hopes of finding my target. "Mr. Calloway?"

"Back here. Just come back." Ah, bingo. A nice, deep voice. Let's go see what's behind door number one.

As I walk towards the door I definitely realize that this day has told me, more than anything else, that I need to get some. When every man pushes my buttons—the good ones, of course—it has to be a sign. Note to self: get some soon.

I make it to the entrance of the door and walk in. Mr. Calloway has his back to me, shuffling papers and prints on his desk. "Hello," I say. "My name is Sarah Sullivan. I'm here to pick up blueprints for my mother, Cindy Sullivan."

Mr. Calloway pivots my way, then stops. No, wait. Did he stop or did I just stop? Because something stopped. Maybe it was my heart. Or my breathing. Or the spinning motion of the earth, because right before me stands none other than Hottie McAngry Pants.

Fuck.

"You have got to be shittin' me!" he spits out. He looks me up and down, stopping a bit too long at my shoes, then works his way back up. I'm gonna be honest, he is a huge prick but his stare-down of me is getting me a bit heated, and not in an angry way. *Hello, Sarah! Back to Earth!* Right... Is this guy for real?

"Excuse me?" is all I can conjure up at this point...again.

"You following me or something?" Now this guy is really just pushing my buttons—and not the good ones. I believe myself to be a calm, nice person (OK, yeah, minus my little office breakdown), but he is about to bring out a whole new side of me.

"Listen, pal," I say. "Trust me, I wouldn't follow you to anywhere. So let's get that straight. And second, I am here to pick up some prints for my mother, which I may add we will be discussing her choice in contractors when I get home!"

"You do that, sweetcakes," he says, turning to go back behind his desk. "I'm perfectly well off to pass on this measly job anyway. No harm here." He tosses the blueprints at me, and I barely catch them before they smack me in the face. This guy is a real treat!

"Well I'm glad we got that out of the way. So continue on your day being a douche and I'll be on my way." I go to turn and he is in front of me before I can even blink. His close proximity to me now is making me a bit flustered.

"Oh don't worry, baby, I'll go on with my day just fine. Now hurry home, I'm sure mommy and daddy are wanting their car back." He is staring at me without an ounce of humor in his tone, then waits for me to start my exit out of his office. When I'm done staring back at him disbelievingly, with the urge to smack him while explaining how I'm not a loser living with my parents—when actually I am a total loser living with my parents—I decide to just bite my lip and move. This is delaying my Golden Girls and I'm sure Aunt Raines is about to go into vermouth arrest in the car.

Stepping to the side and out of Hottie McBig-and-Broad's way, I walk past his office. My final attempt to get the last word is flashing my middle finger while exiting his office but I have a feeling it's been missed by the sound of the door slamming behind my back. For what it's worth, and if anyone asks, I won.

I make it back to the car without being eye-assaulted by the construction models and get the hell outta dodge. After apologizing to Aunt Raines for the delay and promising to take the faster route home, we are on our way. But I still can't believe what just happened in there! When did it become OK to be such a jerk to someone? Do I come off as a slum who doesn't look like they can afford car insurance, or better yet, respect? So I am wearing my infamous T-shirt and sweats. So what? They are my comfort zone. And who doesn't like my shoes? They are golden five-inch stiletto Manolo Blahniks! Ugh.

I sneak a peek in my rearview mirror and do a quick sweep at myself. Finger-brush my hair. Wipe my face with my palm. Not helping. I remind myself to remove all mirrors in my path. I mean, maybe I do deserve to be treated this way. It's not like I've been showing myself any sort of respect lately anyway.

Sadness fuels across my face as I turn onto our block. I just don't know when things got so bad. I try to go back and remember why I couldn't see the signs along the way. Memories flood in: walking into our apartment, searching for where Stacey was, only to find her underneath my boyfriend. My Steve. My one and only Steve of seven years. When did I lose focus and stop seeing the signs? The looks on both their faces when their eyes connected with mine. The attempts they didn't make to deny what was happening and the pleas that they never meant to hurt me. Not sure how my best friend and boyfriend fucking defines as not hurting someone, but, whatever.

It all went downhill fast after that. I flipped my shit at work, telling off Steve in front of the entire board, finishing my erratic scene by announcing that I also quit and then walked out. Not that I would have stayed if I could go back and do it all over again, but Stacey had said it was best we probably did not live together anymore, and since everything was practically hers at that point, I packed up what little was mine and left.

I can't say I ended up on my parents' front step in good shape either. I was devastated. Everything I had worked so hard for was just...gone. Stolen right from under me. One minute I had a great life, with a stunning apartment in the city, a great best friend, a handsome, wonderful boyfriend, and my dream job. Then I blinked and I had nothing.

"You OK, sweetling?"Aunt Raines asks, breaking me from my pathetic thoughts.

"Yeah, I'm just great, Auntie. We're home, no more fretting. Now how about some cocktails?"

"Sure thang, baby. You sure you're OK? Your mamma told me about your bad luck. Shame that man didn't know what he had."

Oh, Aunt Raines, always seeing the bright side of people, of situations. If all else fails, maybe she will let me live with her and help sell her necklaces on the beach. Maybe my destiny is to be a wallflower lacking taste in accessories.

"I'm good, Aunt Raines. Let's go toast to Uncle Merle."

Here, here.

Chapter 4

I am laying on my bed spread-eagle as he slowly makes his way up my legs. I can feel his breath on my skin as he presses his thumbs against my inner thighs. Slowly, he raises his head and speaks my name, but for some reason it sounds off. I continue to focus on his face while he moves his way upward, taking little nibbles on the side of my waist. Again, he says my name. Only this time, I'm not so sure it sounds as seductive as would the typical voice of a hot muscular man who is about to just completely ravish me. *Focus, focus,* I start to scold myself. We are just getting to the good part, and I have a feeling this is going to get *real* good. He makes his way up my stomach and his hands brush against my chest while he dips his head and begins to whisper in my ear, "It's not you..."

"SARAH! Get up!"

This is not happening.

I can't even get some in my dreams! Not only does my dream man have my damn mother's voice, but right before he's going to show me the goods, he starts to break up with me. I really need to get a book on dreams and the psyche. Rolling over to my side, because I have a feeling I may have the female version of blue balls, I take my pillow between my legs and squeeze. I miss a warm body next to me. I miss Steve.

No I don't.

Yes I do.

No. I. Don't.

I don't miss a man who was sleeping with my roommate and best friend for months behind my back. I used to worry it was me. That something was wrong. Steve would tell me nothing, that he was just swamped with work and he had big clients to focus on. He slowly stopped spending the night. Weird to think about it, but so did Stacey. I sometimes wonder if I did see the signs and chose to ignore them. Once I came home to find Stacey and Steve practically in a wrestling position on the floor laughing and joking around. They seemed pretty freaked out when I came home unexpectedly but I didn't think anything of it. They had told me they were just messing around and tripped over the coffee table. I laughed it off with them and offered to make everyone dinner. Man, what a fool I was. And they just let me be one.

"Sarah!"

Ugh, can't a person just lay in bed and wallow in their own self-pity!?

"Yes, Mom?" I attempt to spit out while peeling my tongue from the roof of my mouth.

"Are you able to move some of your things out of the garage and into your room? We need to make some space for the contractor to store some tools while he works."

Wait... Step back a second. Did she just say contractor? Because I'm pretty sure that last night after my fourth martini I verbally expressed my dissatisfaction with her choice in contractors. I had told her it was my new civic duty to help her find a new and better one. I also then passed out on my floor. Which makes me wonder how I'm even in my bed right now. Man, I'm a lightweight. Poor

Aunt Raines probably stayed up and had seven more drinks after I crashed like a virgin college girl.

I make the effort to pull my legs, which may I add feel like dead weight, off the bed. Then I do a sheet check (not this time, floor), and stand up. As the room begins to slowly spin, I attempt to find my sweats. Where are my lucky sweats? My comfort zones? It takes me two tries of eye searching before I find them in the corner babysitting a pile of vomit. Classic, Sarah, classic. Oh hell, who cares? I'm a grown woman and I can walk around in my damn underwear if I want to. It's not like my mother hasn't seen me in many other forms. She did birth me, right?

I walk down the hallway, bypassing the bathroom, because today is not going to be a cleanliness day, and I make my way down the stairs. Turning to my left I enter the kitchen, only to smack right into the one and only Hottie McBulging Biceps. He wraps his strong hands around my shoulders to steady me so I don't go down. Wow, his grip is firm. And delightful. And those arms...

"Honey, you remember Jack Calloway, right?" I think my mother is talking to me but I am lost in thought. Those tanned arms, wrapping their long, strong length around my... "Sarah?"

"Huh??" I snap out of whatever trance I am in. Where was I again? Oh yeah, my kitchen.

In my underwear...

With McHottie...

Wait. What?! It takes about 2.5 seconds to register reality and 2.5 more to make an attempt to turn around to bolt right back upstairs, causing my foot to get caught in the world's oldest and longest telephone cord and thus fall flat on my face. With my shirt halfway up my back.

Death cannot come soon enough for me.

"Honey, oh my! Are you all right?"

As my mother rushes over to help me adjust myself, I scurry to my feet only to see McRude God staring at me with a smirk on his face. "I'm fine, Mom," I manage. "I was just going to take some inventory of the garage. Not sure there's much room to move anything. Probably won't be able to really move anything at all." I say all of this as I stare him up and down, as he is doing to me. Unfortunately his smirk just continues to grow into a devilish grin.

"Well just take a peek, dear. It would really be helpful to Jack if you could."

"Oh I'm sure it would, *Jack*." I give him one last angry squint and proceed to pivot and walk towards the garage.

"Thanks, dear… Oh, and Sarah?"

"Yeah Mom?" I turn back to face my mother, blocking out the handsome McJerk next to her. "Maybe you should put some pants on?"

Maybe in the garage I can start the engine and let the fumes just kill me right there. I am never drinking with Aunt Raines again. I simply nod and continue on my quest.

Chapter 5

I spend two days and a lot of nagging my mother to move my stuff out of the garage and into my room for me, mainly because it takes that long to get rid of my hangover enough to do anything useful. I'm currently in the garage acting like a bratty teenager, stomping and tossing my stuff around in hopes that someone gives in and tells me to leave my stuff alone. I mean, this is ridiculous. Why do I have to move my stuff? I need to find my own place. One that doesn't include having to share space with a particular man.

Speaking of, I haven't had a run-in with McHotstuff since my kitchen show and still this guy has me on edge. I haven't even had any juicy dreams about my hot dream man. Just nightmares about falling face first into the floor with my shirt riding up my back. Oh wait. That was reality... Ugh.

I need to get this guy out of my head, starting by getting him out of my house. I mean, what is my mother thinking anyway!? Didn't I make myself clear the other night? Aunt Raines says I had made a good argument in the beginning, but by my fifth martini it was straight muscles talk and how dreamy his ass looks. I need to not drink with Aunt Raines anymore, and get a backbone.

And take argumentative classes.

Note that to self.

I begin to move some boxes around, only to break the bottom of one open and have all my things dump to the floor. "Seriously?" I hiss. I kick another box, and it of course domino effects and takes out a crate full of tools.

This is just great. I'm bent over to assess the damage, when I hear stomping feet approach.

"What the hell are you doing?!"

I turn to see *him* quickly walking toward me, jaw locked and wearing an impressively angry look.

"Listen, it was an accident," I growl out and dip down in an attempt to pick up his tools.

"Don't touch my equipment!" He swats my hand away and bends down to place his scattered tools back into the overturned crate.

"Listen buddy, it was an accident. Maybe you should find another place to store your junk!"

"Junk, huh?!"

"Yeah, junk—" As I try to finish spitting out my sentence, he bends over and picks up a pair of my shiny stilettos. Dangling my Jimmy Choos over my head, he then proceeds to throw them across the garage.

"What the hell do you think you're doing?" I scream.

"Oh don't worry, sweetheart. I'm just helping you make room for my 'junk'!"

"Oh no you didn't!" I get right in his face. He follows suit which brings us nose to nose, ready to face off. His eyes are flaming orbs and I can feel his breath hitting my cheeks.

"You're going to regret this," I hiss.

"You have no idea." In record speed, he raises his hand and throws it behind my neck, then he grabs my head and slams his mouth on mine. I have been pondering the feel of his mouth pressed against mine for days, but it's nothing like the real thing. Too shocked, I don't know whether to fight him off or wrap my arms around his neck to deepen the kiss. Before I can find out, he releases me.

"Don't touch the equipment," he says, out of breath, and walks out of the garage.

What the hell?

"What the hell?"

I press my fingers to my lips. I can feel them a bit swollen from his aggressive kiss. I want to storm out of here screaming *assault*, but holy hotness that was seriously the hottest kiss I have ever experienced. Who is this guy?!

As I make a pathetic attempt at moving my boxes, I can't get the feel of his mouth out of my mind. One minute, I'm pretty sure he is going to kill me and hide my body under my parents' soon-to-be new addition, then the next minute he is kissing me. Like a man in heat. Like a *hot* wild man in heat. I mindlessly move stuff around, picking up a box, trying not to touch his tools. And all the while, I can't stop thinking about touching his other *'tools'*.

Chapter 6

It has been a week since my last run-in with Hottie McMacho Pants and my hopes are that it continues. As I lay in bed I can hear the trucks coming in and out of the driveway dumping supplies, and voices in and out of the house. The one most stinging is the one of the tall, strong, handsome jerk who keeps invading my head and my dreams. For some insane reason my dreams at night now include the hands of that one man in particular. Why can't I just dream about someone I don't know? So I don't feel so wrong asking for it rough? Instead, in my dream I have McSteamy's hands all over me while he kisses me with need and hunger just as I remember it in the garage. The even more horrid thing is that I am completely enjoying it. I need to check on the status of where I'm at with getting some real action. I should write that task down.

I decide that today is going to be a motivation day. I am going to shower. I am going to shave. I am going to put on my best stilettos and get my highly qualified ass a job. My parents are right. I have a great degree. And I am hugely talented. I didn't work at the biggest marketing firm and under the most highly respected clients in the business to not be good at what I did. Too bad seven years of the hardest work I have ever performed ended in a seven-minute blowout freak show.

Well...moving on. First plan of action is to find a coffee shop and pump myself with caffeine, then search the wanted ads. I'm feeling good about this. Positive. Can't say I've had this much motivation in quite some time. I get out of bed, sheet free (I'm catching on). I head for the shower. Not going to lie, it's been a while since I've primped so I make sure to swap out the semi-used can of shaving cream for a full bottle. There's definitely some work to be done in there.

Having hot water hit my face feels glorious. I actually forgot how good it feels to stand under the hot water and let all the day's wear and tear melt away. I remember how Steve and I would work late together, then head back to his condo, order takeout then jump in his gigantic shower, and just stand there holding each other while making love until we were pruned and our legs were shaking. He would wash my hair and caress me while leaning over me and being gentle with every scrub of my body. He would pat me dry and place me in his big T-shirts while we ate our takeout and discussed our latest clients and projects. I thought that was perfect. I thought things were exactly how they were supposed to be. I was so wrapped up in my perfect world that I never took the time to even question or realize then why one night I spotted one of Stacey's hair bands on his counter. The things you know now that you wish you knew then.

Quickly deciding that showering is way overrated, I opt that a quick one is better. As the water turns tepid, I also now confirm I hate showers. I mean, it's a simple task, why do people make such a big deal of it? Wash, scrub, shave, and get out. People waste too much time in this—

"HOLY!—"

What the...

Just then, cold water starts spurting straight at my face. I attempt to quickly scrub the remaining shampoo out of my hair. While dodging ice splatter, I throw myself out of the shower, of course slipping right off the mat and onto the floor. What is the obsession with my face wanting to connect with the floor?! Pulling myself up, I try to get my eyes to stop burning since I have shampoo seeping in them. I focus on my current state of mayhem, grab the nearest towel and barrel out the door.

"Mom!" I scream because there is no way she forgot to pay the water bill. "MOM! Why is the hot water not working? I was in the middle of—"

Oomph! Walking into the living room and slamming right into a hard hot body was not what I was expecting. As I look up while adjusting to my foam-glazed vision, I see Sexy McTouch Me staring at me with that damn grin again.

"How did you get in here?! Where is my mother?" I spit out angrily, trying to look around for my mother while preparing for the lecture of a lifetime on how she has to stop letting this hunk of a man into our home!

"She left it open for me. We are starting the addition today. We had to turn the water heater off to get the wires under the old deck," he explains with a hint of humor. God, I hate this man.

"Well you could have warned us that you were shutting it off. Some people were actually using that hot water!" I state as rudely as I possibly can while not staring at the day-old stubble lining his oh-so-attractive jawline. "You interrupted my hot shower, you know!"

"I can see that." He dips down to my feet and stands up, handing me what looks like—are you flipping kidding me— my towel.

I storm back up the stairs listening to the chuckle echoing behind me, then I slam the door to the bathroom shut and press myself against it. Bashing my head against the door, I attempt to wake myself up, 'cause this just cannot be happening to me. Two times now, Mr. McSeductive Eyes has seen my goods and not in a willing, would-you-like-to-touch-me kind of see my goods. Don't get me wrong, I have goods to show, but I'm slowly starting to feel like this guy was sent to finish me off. If my life slipping from right under me like a tacky 70s rug was not enough, let's send Mr. McDo Me Sideways to complete the job.

Things are not looking good for me and my emotional psyche. Someone out of this is going to be paying for my therapy bills. Note to self: definitely find a therapist.

Chapter 7

I've always thought of myself as a lucky person. I thought when I left college with that degree still warm in my hands that I was destined to become something great. I pinned myself as an independent, willing to go out in the world on my own and become a person of greatness. I would see an opportunity and indulge in it until I owned it. Now I look back and wonder when I became this person that missed that drive. When did I lose who I was and fall into the background of what others were becoming? I try to think of when exactly things started to crumble in front of me. When did Steve stop seeing me as his only one? When did Stacey look at me and not see enough love and trust to turn away from my boyfriend? When did I decide I wasn't that girl who loved wearing her converses and hoodies and drinking beer and I swapped it out for the life of heels, fancy clothes and cocktail dinners? When did I stop being me?

I dig through the boxes to find my Prada wedges and Fendi wrap about two seconds after I decide that I am not going soul searching. Luckily enough the next box over has my old green converses in it, which happen to go great with my old-school Lucky jeans. Maybe tomorrow will be the day. Today, just coffee. It's all about getting back on the horse. Albeit slowly. Because I'm not sure anyone got back on the horse without caffeine.

I walk out of the house and slam my oversized sunglasses on my face. The sun is shining and birds are chirping and I am coffee-less and not in the mood. I bee-line it for the Stabbin Wagon hoping not to run into my nemesis. One could only hope, right?

"So I see you were able to get the rest of the shampoo out of your hair."

One. Could. Only. Hope.

I turn to see Macho McSnuggly Arms walk towards me while wiping off his hands with a rag. "Well thanks to you, it was a cold process," I reply like any mature twelve-year-old would.

"Listen," he says. "I'm sorry we got off on the wrong foot. The accident. I was late for an appointment. Funny enough it was to meet you. I'm sorry." Well, that was not what I was expecting. He continues. "I owe you a phone. If you want, I'm letting the crew take a break here and need to head up to my site for some supplies. If you want to join me we can stop by a phone store and I can replace your phone."

I would have responded if I wasn't too busy just staring at him with my mouth open in utter shock. Who is this guy standing in front of me? I want desperately to tell him where he can shove his gesture and apology, but then the image of him and shoving turns into me thinking about his strong legs around me, shoving...

"So is that a yes or are you just going to stand there and stare at me all day?"

"Oh… Um… Well, I was just…" What was I just going to do again? Oh yeah, act like a human! "Well, I was just going to get some coffee. I guess it would be all right, as long as we can stop at a caffeine pump so I can fill up."

As he now stares back a little thrown off, he adjusts his raised eyebrows and says, "Sure. There's a Starbucks on the way."

I nod an "OK" and start walking with him toward his truck. What am I doing? I have a feeling this is not a good idea. He is probably luring me in with his strong arms and even bigger shoulders so he can finish me off, and not in a good way. I'm leading myself into my own death. I just know it. I hope he at least feeds me my coffee first.

"So I guess maybe a proper introduction would work here too, huh?" He reaches out his hand to me and says, "I'm Jack Calloway." I extend my hand and our palms glide together in a slow handshake. My body temperature instantly rises, and I can feel my palm getting sweaty against his. What is wrong with me? I pull away because this instant friction is weirding me out and since I can feel my cheeks warming, I'm sure he notices it too.

"Oh yeah," I stutter. "Sarah Sullivan"

"Nice to properly meet you, Sarah Sullivan. Let me go release my guys and then we can get you fueled and back into the world of technology."

I nod and watch Jack (kind of weird using his real name) dismiss his crew and head back over to his truck. "You ready?" he asks, then directs me towards the passenger side of his big manly truck. He opens the door for me and I hesitate a bit.

I am not too sure how someone of my stature is supposed to climb into this massive vehicle. As I pivot and begin to lift one leg to reach the stepping base, Jack grabs my waist and boosts me into the seat. *Oh, lordie.* "Um. Thanks." I try not to make eye contact because at this point I'm probably as flushed as a tomato. Was I just blushing? Who am I? I mean, just because I can still feel his fingers pressed against my sides, there is no reason to blush like a fifteen-year-old girl. *So get a hold of yourself, Sarah...* And your libido.

Once I'm settled in, Jack rounds the truck and jumps in, pulls it from the curb and gears down the street with ease. As we hit the first light out of the neighborhood, Jack's phone starts ringing. "Jack Calloway," he answers. He looks professional and comfortable in his little work bubble. Sitting so close and assessing his motions is starting to make my skin boil. For the first time I am actually getting a good look at him, and watching him speak with ease to a client about what sounds like a big project is totally turning me on. He is kind and so businesslike with his feedback. He spits out some numbers and dimensions like it's already sitting on his tongue. I observe his mouth move while his fingers glide over the steering wheel with gentle yet assertive force. *Hmmmm... Those fingers.* Did I just catch myself licking my lips?

"Thank you," he says. "I will have the foreman on the site retrieve the fax. Great. We'll be in touch." He shuts his phone off and sets it back on the dash. "I'm sorry about that. This phone seems to be ringing nonstop lately."

"Oh. Um, no worries," I say. "So...Calloway Construction. Is this all yours or is it a family business?"

"It was my father's, but he died in an accident a couple years back. I had been working for him for a few years when the accident happened, then everything went to me.

I jumped in the hot seat and have been running it ever since."

"Oh my god, I'm so sorry! I didn't mean to—"

"Oh no, it's OK. Long time ago."

I settle back into my chair a little less comfortable. What an ass. I mean, who brings up something like that at a time like this? Probably sensing my uncomfortableness, Jack starts in again. "So, Sarah, what do you do?"

Ugh. Wrong question. "Uhh, nothing at the moment. I'm in-between jobs. I decided to take a leave from what I was doing. Find something else," I say, not sounding confident at all in my explanation.

Probably feeling the awkwardness in the air, he changes the subject. "So what kind of phone did I decide to let die in the middle of Waverly Street?" he says, slowly grinning and looking my way. Wow, those eyes. I used to think they were a hazel color. Because I cared or something and I was not having dreams about those eyes. To my mistake they are actually more of a gold color. He looks at me with a sexy gaze, waiting for me to respond.

"You know, the average smart phone, with all the latest accessories. It was fully stocked with music and apps."

Jack chuckles at my stab at humor. "We will just have to see then," he replies and then pulls into Starbucks.

After Jack helps me climb out of his beast-mobile, we walk up to the Starbucks. He opens the door and tells me to go ahead of him. Gotta respect a man with chivalry. We walk up to the counter, with a few people in front of us while we stare at the menu. Not that I need a review of what a coffee place has to offer. Let's be honest. I just don't know where else to look. I don't need to look at Jack to feel the heat that is pouring off of him. Or is it me? Either way, I'm not sure drinking coffee and adding any more adrenaline to my already on-fire body is such a good idea after all. I am seriously considering decaf.

"You sure are studying that menu." Jack breaks my train of thought.

"Um, who me? Yeah, you can never be too sure. They add stuff all the time. Gotta keep my options open." Oh. My. God. Shut up now. I sound like a babbling moron.

Jack just laughs and rolls his eyes. Once the customers in front of us put in their orders, Jack gently presses his hand against my back to guide me forward.

"Welcome to Starbucks. What can I get you today?" Is it wrong to order an ice water right now, then ask this tweener girl cashier to dump it on my head?

"Yeah, I'll take a Grande Caramel Mocha with skim milk, double shot espresso in a Venti cup, and add extra whip cream. Thanks." The girl just stares at me. They always do! What? I'm a paying customer and sugar is just as important as caffeine. She reluctantly types in my order and adjusts her eyes to the next paying customer. I see her eyes wrap behind me and lock on Jack. As in not being obvious AT ALL! Seriously? This guy can be my boyfriend and tweener-bop over here is openly just gawking at him! How rude! Then, in her lamest attempt to sound seductive, she asks Jack what his order will be. Amazingly enough, he doesn't seem to take note of her flirtatiousness. He simply spits out his order for a large black coffee and proceeds to dig in his wallet to pay.

"Oh here, I can pay for mine—" I start to say, but he cuts me off.

"It's on me. The least I can do."

I'm not entirely sure what the "most" he could do is, but if he is offering I might have a few ideas—

"Sarah! Is that you?" Catching me off guard, I turn to my right and dead center in my line of vision is Becky Longhorn. Otherwise known as Steve Hamilton's big-mouthed secretary. Also known as the victim in the formerly mentioned Freak-Out Show in which I took his plant and tossed it Olympic-style at Steve, barely missing Becky's head.

"Becky, wow, nice to see you," I choke out, wishing that at this exact moment a bomb goes off in this specific Starbucks, killing me first. "What are you doing all the way out here in the suburbs?"

"Oh, we are out here doing some baby registry shopping. You know Bill, it's so hard to get him away from the office to do anything and we have our little bundle of joy coming so soon!" she squeals, while taking the opportunity to lift her hands and obnoxiously rub at her growing belly.

"Wow, that's great. Beautiful maternity dress, by the way." I watch her scrunch her nose at my comment because I'm pretty sure that is nothing close to a maternity dress and I just got one in on little ole' Becky. Seeing Bill back up a bit, I'm pretty sure he's going to feel the wrath of that later. Sorry, Bill. "When's the little squirt due?" I ask because I seriously care. Not.

"Just a little more than eight months!" Eight months?! I believe a bit of a snort escapes my lips. Talk about early planning. At eight months, doesn't that make someone, like, *just* pregnant?

I'm taking bets in my head that Becky is divorced in twelve months, when her squawking voice brings me back to reality. "Bill says…" Ugh. Bill, who cares about Bill? I'm not sure he has had his own personal opinions since he met Becky. Poor Bill. Maybe I would be doing him a favor as well with the whole bomb thing. We can only hope.

Just as Jack walks up behind me with our coffees, Becky does what she does best and chimes in. "Anywho, you know I'm really sorry about what happened with you and Steve and the job. Everyone was so shocked to hear the sad news. I mean, well, those who didn't witness it. But who would have thought? Steve and Stacey!?" What are the chances Jack has suddenly gone deaf? Since Becky doesn't know when to stop, she just goes on. "We really miss you at the office. It was hard after you left. No one ever did your job like you. They found a replacement shortly after you left but she doesn't work as hard as you did."

Because spending the rest of my life in prison for strangling her fat mouth is not an option, I put a killer smile on my face, and I mean *killer* because it is literally painful to be smiling at this point and not either A. crying, or B. throwing up.

"Yeah, who would have thought? Well I'm glad they've replaced me. Wouldn't want the company stuck in the mud without work being done." Just as I finish choking out my sentence, I feel Jack's heat emanating from behind me. He gently brushes his hand against my lower back and hands me my coffee with his other hand.

"Oh my! Sarah, who is this? I didn't know you had a brother!"

OK, that's it!

"Hey. Jack." Jack introduces himself with a head nod, then turns my direction and wraps his arm around my waist and places his body very close to my side. He slowly leans into me and presses a soft kiss to my neck.

Becky is practically drooling. "Oh, well hello there, Jack."

"Babe, you ready to go?" Jack pulls his head away from my neck and locks eyes with me. For a second I am not quite paying attention because I don't even realize it's me he's talking to.

"Oh yeah. I'm all good. Let's go. Well Becky, for real, great seeing you. Hope we can make this a reoccurring event." I barely finish my sentence before I start walking towards the door. Jack is right on my heels, still pressing his hand behind my lower back. I toss the door open and try to suck the air into my lungs. I am not looking forward to a breakdown in the middle of a Starbucks parking lot, but with my luck lately it seems inevitable.

"You OK?" Jack asks.

"Oh yeah, just fine," I say while speed-walking to his truck. We reach the passenger's side and he steps forward to help boost me up, but I need no help since I have adrenaline pumping through my ears. I pretty much jump into the seat. He shuts my door, walks around and gets in, and starts the truck. Then he turns towards me. I'm pretty sure he's assessing how safe it is to speak.

"Do you want to talk about it?" he asks.

I'm not sure what there is to talk about. Somehow it all pours out anyway.

"I think Becky pretty much spilt my beans. Girl has perfect job, perfect boyfriend, and perfect friend. Perfect life. One day girl walks into perfect apartment and catches perfect boyfriend in bed with perfect friend. Girl then proceeds to make an incredible scene at perfect job where she works with perfect boyfriend, then she quits her perfect job. Now perfect girl is not so perfect and is camping out in her parents' house while waiting for the world to end so she doesn't have to get back out in it... Did you get all that?"

He is quiet for a moment, and then he says, "Sarah, I'm sorry."

I raise my hand. "Don't... Just don't, OK? I don't need your sympathy, all right? Just...just take me home."

We drive back in silence and all I can do is think about how pathetic I must have looked just now. Here I am judging Jack the whole time of being this big McJerk and look who turns out to be the pathetic one. They replaced me at work. I'm not going to deny that I was stalking the job posting that went up not twenty-four hours after my theatrics, or how the position was filled two days later.

Seven years of my life I gave that company and they just fill my position with someone in a seventy-two hour time span. I kind of thought they would look past my outburst. Give me some time and ask if I would return. Possibly threaten to demote me due to my unprofessionalism, at worst. I thought I meant something to that company. Apparently I was just another number to them, making them tons of money. I was easily replaced. Just like that. It hurts to know I wasn't worth fighting for. In my work nor in my relationship. Steve didn't bother fighting to keep me; he just let me go. He agreed this was for the best. And Stacey wouldn't even look at me to fight for our friendship. She obviously chose the latter. And the latter was not me.

I snap out of my misery-induced coma-like state to realize we are parked in my driveway. Jack has been sitting there quietly, assessing me again. I don't look his way. I open the door and climb out of his truck. I walk with a bit of a hustle towards the house, hoping he will just let me go in and pretend this day never happened. Then, as I reach the door and turn slowly to face him, I notice he is practically touching me, he's that close. He stands just inside my personal space with his hands resting deep inside his front pockets. Due to our height difference I look up and my eyes lock directly with his lips. I can't help but remember that soft but luscious kiss he pressed to my neck at Starbucks. Subconsciously, I bring my fingers to my neck, where I can still feel the heat of his mouth against my skin. I lift my eyes to meet his. He stares at me intensely, as if contemplating my next move.

"Hey Jack, thanks for playing hot wingman back there," I say as nonchalantly as possible. "I really appreciate it. Hopefully it gives Becky something to gossip about for the next week." What I should be doing is throwing myself at him, not talking.

"Sure," he says quietly as he looks at me with sadness in his eyes. I give him the goodbye head nod and turn to trek inside. Jack lets me go.

No sadness here. The last thing I need is for anyone to feel sorry for me. I'm a big girl. I can handle this. I'm totally fine, actually. So I don't know why I make it to my room just in time to shut the door and fall flat on my bed right before the dam of waterworks explodes and sends me drowning in my sorrow.

Chapter 8

Guessing by the shadow coming from my window and the crusted drool sticking to the side of my face, I assume that I have been sleeping for a while. Crying like a five-year-old who's been denied ice cream can really wear a person out. I sit up and scope out my room. First thing first: Search out that coffee. Now I know I am a waste of good looks at this point but a perfectly good latte should not pay the price. I find my neglected cup sitting on a makeshift desk made out of boxes. I sip the liquid goodness, hoping to get bits and pieces of whip cream (oh yeah, best part) and fail miserably. Then I proceed to exit my Home Shopping Network cave.

I've come to the realization that I need to make a list. Don't people make lists at my age? To-do lists? Bucket lists? Things they want to conquer before they die? On the fast train of public humiliation that I am on, my time has to be nearing soon. Might as well start making some plans before I dispose of my good-looking self into the abyss of death. I head for the kitchen in pursuit of some writing materials. When I enter, I find good ole' Aunt Raines preparing for happy hour—already.

"Hey there, sweet girl. I thought you were never gonna get up," Aunt Raines says. I scoop a pen and some scrap paper out of the junk drawer and proceed to sit at the table next to her makeshift bar. "What are you up to, sweet Sarah?"

"Oh you know, Aunt Raines, just trying to find the meaning of life."

She scoots closer to me with her shaker. "Well you have come to the right place, dear. Your Uncle Merle would always sit me down with a full glass in hand and tell me that there were always answers at the bottom of a glass of happiness."

"Uncle Merle said this?" I state a bit shocked.

"Oh he sure did, sweet girl. Every time I would get into a tiff with life or upset over something silly, he would sit me down, shake me up some happiness and tell me to sit it out while I sip on it."

"Huh," I say, trying to ponder this theory and also imagining my Uncle Merle feeding every problem with a glass of stiff vermouth. Did I mention that my uncle had been a minister at a church for seventeen years?

"So what was the outcome? Did you find the answers you were looking for?"

"Well most of the time, no. But I did find a really good buzz and in the end it didn't matter what I was up in a rut about, because after a few sips to warm my blood I would relax and realize that life is what you make of it. If you take it too seriously you just end up injuring your own self."

Why do I not spend more time with my Aunt Raines? Her words are so simple but so true. Why was I taking everything that went wrong so hard? Why do I feel like the decisions that other people make around me or for me define who I am? I am not the cheater or the betrayer. I'm the victim. But who wants to be the victim either? I just want to be me again. I want to be happy about something. Accomplishments that I earned. I want to look forward and not to my past. I want my past to be just that—my past.

As I finish my first martini, I begin to write. After I finish my third one though, I am scribbling. "Aunt Raines, what would you do if you were in my position?"

"Well what position are you in, babycakes?"

It takes me just a second to think of exactly how to word it. "My life is in a rut right now and I don't know how to get out of it." Because it feels like I do but in a way I don't. I feel like if I knew what to do, I would have done it by now.

"Well sweet Sarah, you need to think about what you find so stuck. People have life altering things happen to them all the time. Some turn out to be for the better. Maybe if you give it time you will see it that way."

I can't say I feel too confident with that advice, but I guess I'll take it. It beats my own advice to myself, and that is to stick my head in the toilet and flush in hopes of a quick and easy death by drowning.

"Thanks, Aunt Raines. I feel better."

"No problem, sweet girl. Now, how about another glass of happiness?"

A genuine smile crosses my face for the first time in ages and I offer her my glass. "Fill her up."

Chapter 9

Now, I am not sure how much happiness Uncle Merle would offer Aunt Raines, but four glasses of pure happiness later and I am as warm as could be on a summer day wrapped up in the arms of a hot construction worker. Or whomever. Construction worker doesn't mean anything or anyone specifically. What is it with me and hitting my four-drink limit before my mind and my libido turn straight down McJack-me-up lane? I just keep finding myself, when not thinking about pathetic topics, a.k.a. my life, gravitating towards him. His smile. The way he lavished my mouth in the garage. The way he caressed my back at the coffee house. His sexy mouth pressed against my neck. The way he gazed at me on the front step with that look of concern and thoughtfulness. I wonder what it would be like to kiss that concern right off his mouth. How he would taste, again. His arms wrapped around my waste while I hold on tighter to his strong arms, and...

"Hey..."

Huh?

Swimming out of the gutter – or out of the bottom of my martini – I begin to refocus on the large object in front of me.

"You're looking better than earlier today," he says. I was looking bad before? Oh yeah: Insert coffee house disaster. Good of him to remember that.

"Yeah. Sorry about that. Things are actually looking up now," I state, slurring a bit into my glass.

"I can see that. And how is that so?" he asks.

"Aunt Raines over here has suggested that all of the answers are at the bottom of this bottle of vermouth. We're making martinis." I turn to Aunt Raines and tilt my martini glass in a salute. As I start to giggle, Aunt Raines begins to stand.

"Well now," Aunt Raines says, "I think it's time for me to wrap it up. I have all the answers I need. I'm going to see what your mamma is up to. I'll just leave you two kids alone." She sets down her glass and turns to me while winking, then sees herself out of the kitchen. What a bad wingman. Leaving me to fend for myself.

"Do you mind if I sit?"

Sure, in my lap. "Nope."

"What's this?" he asks, grabbing at the rough draft of my bucket list. I half attempt to swat it out of his hands because A) I hardly even remember what it says, but I fail because B) It takes too much effort. I'm lacking effort nowadays. I don't even think I like vermouth.

"So, is this some sort of list?" he asks with a hint of humor in his tone.

"You can say that. I figure it's about time I wake up and get out of my parents' house. I've been here for almost four months now, ya know?" *Did I just admit that?*

Kill me now.

"So what's stopping you?" he says. *Man, this guy's good.*

"Nothing is stopping me. I'm still trying to figure things out. Where my place is. Maybe I don't want to go back to a fancy firm with fancy people and fancy things," I say defensively, probably more to myself than to Jack.

Maybe that life was never meant for me in the first place. When I got my degree in Marketing, I wanted to build ads and create powerful logos that stuck with people, that made a difference. I wanted to draw architecture and create billboard ads. I wanted to feel good about a product I was selling and feel honest about the message I was sending across. I felt that way in the beginning of Hamilton Corp. All the fresh faces and challenging projects. I would complete one to jump right into another, knowing that the drive and competition were just part of the thrill. But in the end, it was never fulfilling. I was never able to create an ad and feel homely about it. In the end it was all about selling the client and locking in the highest bidder.

Jack starts reading my list, and he begins to chuckle. "What is so funny?" I snap at him, trying and again failing at swatting back my list.

"Number one - Make a list," he recites out loud while laughing.

"Yeah, make a list! You have to start somewhere, don't you?"

His laughter softens. "You are correct."

He reads on, stopping only to look at me for clarification. "Number two - Plan life."

"Yes. It's probably important to try and build some sort of path or direction."

"Ok… Number three - Fulfill a goal." Again he stops to look at me.

"*Fulfill a goal*. I want to set my mind to something and complete it. I've always loved to read. I used to love reading books when I was younger. Lose myself in sappy romance novels. I never do it anymore. I don't know, maybe I'll finish 100 books by the end of the year."

"You know it's already June, right?"

"Yeah. You're right. OK, cross that one off."

"OK, moving on. Number four - Find out what else is at the end of the tunnel." This time he looks at me in amusement. "Care to elaborate?"

"Why does everyone always say there is light at the end of the tunnel? So what? What else is there? What if the light isn't good enough for me? I don't want to settle for just light, ya know?" We look at each other and lock eyes for some time. I can see the understanding in his eyes. He is agreeing with me. Sometimes there needs to be more than just light.

"I will take that. Next, number five - Find myself, on a budget." His eyebrows shoot up as he looks at me again.

"Exactly what it says, Jackie boy. Find myself. Go in search of who I really am but in an unemployed and on a budget sort of way. You know those people who travel the world trying to figure out where their place is? I want to do that but possibly in this particular suburb, and under twenty bucks."

Jack just laughs. He doesn't even try to hold this one in. He simply belts out a huge gust of laughter. His laugh singing in my ears is so infectious, it makes my legs squeeze together. Who is this man? And why is he sitting in my kitchen with me all gorgeous and edible and laughing like some Greek god? "You're staring," he says when his laughter softens.

Huh? "Huh? Oh, no I'm not."

"Yes you were…"

"Listen, don't think so highly of yourself, pal."

"All right, all right. Moving on. Number six - Remember what falling in love feels like." He finishes the last of that sentence in almost a whisper. His laughter dies down even more and he turns to look at me. I, on the other hand, am staring at my glass. The mood has gotten a bit more serious than I had planned and I'm pretty sure the fun is over. I turn to wrap this party up, and catch Jack holding me in his gaze, waiting intensely for a response. "Care to clarify?"

Not really. Stupid vermouth.

"Well, exactly what it says. It's been a while since I can remember that feeling. The one with the butterflies and the sleepless nights because all you can do is think about the one who has your heart. The warmness you feel when he touches you. When things were real. When it was only you he had eyes for and you can even see that love burning in his eyes…"

At this point I think I just drifted. I'm not even sure I'm really talking to anyone anymore. Why would I even write that? Why would I even care? Love is such a foolish thing to want anyway. So in the end you can be crushed and made a fool? To wake up one day and realize that it was all a one-man show, and suddenly your better half becomes your roommate's? To feel such emotion for another person and for them to rip it away and take advantage of your heart? To not even care enough to be honest... To just end up leaving you in the end?

I don't realize that Jack at some point had moved from his chair and is now kneeling in front of me. Nor do I realize that at some point I had started to cry.

With Jack being a gigantic six-foot-two compared to my puny 5'4" frame, when he kneels in front of me his head is level with mine. He takes his hand and gently wipes the tear that's spilling down my cheek. I attempt to open my mouth to say something but nothing comes out. I am done.

I'm waving my white flag. I just can't talk about how sad I am anymore to anyone. I attempt to push him away so I can get up and flee, but he puts his hands on each side of me face and holds me there. I try to look away out of shame that I have even opened up about such a pitiful issue, and then proceed to cry about it.

"I'm sorry, I didn't mean—" I begin, but he hushes me with his finger over my lips. Without breaking eye contact, he leans in closer and touches his lips to mine. His breath hits my lips like a warm summer breeze. His lips are soft and gentle and inviting. I sit there a bit tense and shocked at his bold move, but I quickly relax in his embrace. He slowly caresses my lips with his own until I feel my hands move upward to wrap around his neck. Giving him the green light, he intensifies the kiss while smoothly opening my mouth with his tongue. Tasting and feeling and brushing his tongue, his lips continue to crush into mine. I feel my grasp around his neck tighten. Before I start to choke him, he breaks away from me and both of us gasp for air. I just stare at him. He speaks first.

"I'm so sorry. I should not have done that."

Umm... That's not what I was hoping he would say.

"Oh," I say. No doubt he is seeing the hurt in my facial expression. No hiding that one.

"No, that's not what I meant... I meant..." Before he can finish, I push him back and attempt to stand.

"No, it's cool, buddy, no hard feelings. I know how that stuff goes, get lost in the moment feeling sorry for the girl." I feel my anger quickly rise. I try to push him further away from me but he catches my wrist.

"No, that's not what I meant," he says. "Look at me." He holds my wrist firmly in his grip, waiting for me to stop fighting his hold and make eye contact with him. This just isn't happening to me. "Sarah, look at me," he says again, and at the sound of my name leaving his lips I turn and look. I see scorching gold eyes burning right into mine. Intense emotions drain out of his eyes and pour into mine. "I didn't kiss you because I felt sorry for you. I kissed you because I haven't stopped thinking about kissing you since I first saw you on the street. Then the second chance I got after you walked into my office all bent out of hell to drive me insane. I haven't slept a good fuckin' night since I slammed my mouth on yours two weeks ago. What I'm sorry about is that I took advantage of you in a vulnerable moment. It was wrong of me."

Oh, for the love…

"Excuse me?" is all that comes out of my mouth because my brain isn't really working anymore.

"I said I can't stop thinking about how it would feel to have my mouth on yours again, ever since that day in the garage."

Holy mother of holy. "Is this really happening?" I have to ask it. I have to know if in about two seconds he is going to whisper in my ear how it's not me…

"I think it's my turn to say, excuse me?" he responds in a confused but humorous way.

I'm not sure if it's the vermouth or the way my whole body is tingling, but boy does this guy have me speechless. I can't even think of anything to retort back. But whoever made the decision, it is now set. Without blinking, I swing my arms out again, around his neck, and crush my lips to his. He wraps his arms around my waist and our bodies slam together. He swops me up from the chair, then he stands holding my weight effortlessly and presses my body into the wall next to where I was just sitting. His mouth is so hot and inviting to the touch. His taste, oh boy, he tastes good. I can't get enough. Will I ever get enough?

Just as he starts to work his way down my neck, I hear the back door open and slam against the wall. Jack drops me from his grasp and we break apart faster than lightning speed to swiftly turn and see my mother walking in with two large paper bags full of groceries. Thank the gods above, they are so full she can't even see over her bags.

"Honey, is that you? Thank goodness. Please help me with these bags. I about bumped into every wall making it into the house."

I back away quickly from Jack and grab a full bag out of her hands. Once her vision is clear she takes in the scene before her. "Oh hello, Jack. I didn't see you there. Is everything OK?"

I respond with force before Jack can say anything. "Yeah, Mom. He was just coming in for a glass of water." I look at Mom then look at Jack who seems to be a bit caught off guard, not to mention winded.

"Oh, that's nice of you dear." As she sets the other bag down on the counter, she turns around and looks at us both, assessing. "Well honey, aren't you going to get him some water? I'm sure he has work to do."

Oh yeah, water... "Right." I turn and trip over my own foot as I stumble to the sink. I open the cupboard and grab for the nearest glass, and two others come falling out at me. I'm completely staying cool right now... Not. I ignore my mom's curious glances and continue my task. While filling the cup, I stare at Jack's reflection in the window. While Mom turns her head to put away groceries, I notice him adjust himself. *Whoa...* Did not expect that. Sexy McKiss-a-lot seems a little affected by our make-out session. I mean, who wouldn't though, making out like teenagers in my parents' kitchen?

More interruptions. "Hey, Boss." A tall attractive blonde sticks his head in through the back kitchen door. "We could use a hand with the shutter boards," he says.

Jack pulls himself together. "Yeah, sure, I'll be right there," he says, then he turns to me and says, "Thanks," and he walks out the back door.

Wow... I simply think while I proceed to chug the glass of water in my hand.

"Honey, wasn't that for Jack?" my mother asks in complete confusion. I just continue drinking.

Chapter 10

Whelp, where to go from here? I will admit that I have a whole new burst of energy, because I most definitely do. But it's also dinner time and I have a martini hangover starting to invite itself into my scull. I debate going to bed in hopes of finishing that little episode with Jack in my dreams. But how about we take a step back first and figure out what the hell just happened in there. I mean, one minute I was sitting there crying like a pathetic loser, and the next minute I was embraced in Jack's arms playing tonsil hockey with him. And possibly the best game I've ever played, may I add. I can't deny the sparks that seemed to electrocute my senses while we kissed. I can still feel my swollen lips tingling. I touch my fingers to my lips while replaying the motions in my head. Somehow, I make it up to my room without bumping into any walls since the only thing I see is my own homemade movie playing in front of me. I shut my door and lean against the cold wood. *Sigh.*

Double sigh.

I notice banging and shuffling of tools and equipment out back, and peel myself off the door to walk towards the window and take a peak. I spot Jack immediately and watch as he talks while pointing to some of the equipment, instructing his men on what to do.

I stand leaning on the window while I watch him work. The way his strong muscles stretch and firm while maneuvering his equipment. The way the sun hits his face and sweat gathers over his forehead. I watch him wipe away a bead of sweat dripping down his face, and grab for his tools with extensive force. *Holy mother of hotness, what kind of man is this?*

I can't stop watching him work, and admire his skills for the job. His strong rough hands maneuvering heavy materials. Lifting wood boards half my weight with such ease. Steve didn't have rough hands at all. I think Steve had softer hands than I did, in fact. Growing up with money, and having everyone care for him, I don't think he had ever even lifted a finger of his own.

Jack moves out of my line of vision and like that vermouth, I simply cannot get enough. Trying to get a better look, I climb over a few boxes and adjust myself to get into a perfect lean-into position between the dresser and box tower. Just watching him is making me sweat. He's using his hands in ways I wouldn't mind having all over me like that. Maybe we can turn this into a little 'you touch yourself, I touch myself' demonstration. I ponder this idea while I attempt to get a bit more comfortable against the ledge, debating how well I can adjust my hand movements while hanging halfway off a window ledge. Then, just as I start making the simple attempt of skimming my fingers down my belly, Jack stops. He lifts his shirt just over his naval to wipe off the sweat above his lip, revealing—

"Oh mother of abs!"

SPLAT!

And… man down.

If a 125 pound, semi intoxicated, totally turned on human could have made a bigger commotion while slipping off the dresser and taking a face tumble five feet to the ground, I would be impressed. I even manage to knock over my box tower all while kicking the lamp into the window, causing it to shatter, and of course, I end my fall by splitting my pants straight down the rear on the way down.

Such is the life of Sarah Sullivan. May we take a short commercial break while I ponder 101 ways to disappear?

I hear people scurrying around downstairs, most likely to come to my aid. Maybe if I just keep my eyes closed they will assume that I am sleeping. People sleep in odd positions, so why would this be any different?

"Sarah, oh my, what happened!?" My mother rushes to my side. Followed by Aunt Raines, dear old Dad, and I believe, Jack. At this time I refuse to open my eyes.

"I think she knocked herself out," I hear my father say, while Aunt Raines chimes in. "Poor baby girl, did you split your pants?"

Remind myself to kill her while managing to take myself out, too. "Honey, say something. Are you OK?"

I am not sure how much longer I can play dead for, but I plan on giving it a try. I can feel all the shadows hanging over me. They should get bored of the scene soon enough and move on with their day.

See? In no time, I can sense them moving and the light peering over my closed eyelids. Finally... *Oomph. What the hell?* "What the hell?" My eyes fly open to witness Jack...*scooping me up in his arms!*

"Honey." My mother's voice again. "What were you doing in here that you knocked over all those boxes and broke your lamp shade?"

Just then I witness all their minds spinning in unison, along with Jack's, and it seems they all put two and two together. Slowly Jack turns to me, still in his arms, grinning.

"Did something catch your eye, Sarah?"

Oh god, did it.

"No," I say, not at all convincingly.

Jack carries me to the bed and gently lays me down, his fingerprints burning into my sides. I can see my mother looking out the window. "Honey, what were you looking at?" Oh god, just kill me!

"Nothing, I'm fine! Everyone get out!" Two more seconds with him this close to me and everyone in the room is going to get more than what they bargained for. Jack included.

"Well I hope you are OK, dear. Looks like you took quite a tumble."

Still holding me, Jack leans in. Feeling his breath on my neck, I hear him say, "Are you sure you're OK?"

I try swatting his hands away from me. "I'm fine," I say quite breathlessly.

As he lets me go and adjusts himself upward, everyone else takes that as a cue to begin their exit. Jack gives me a wink as he turns to exit my room.

"Honey, well at least since your pants are ruined you may want to wear something more...yourself?" My mother smiles at me and walks out. Avoiding it until now, I look down and see that my comfort zone pants are ruined. Split wide open and revealing a nice pair of purple underwear. Well, at least there's that.

I decide to lay low for the rest of the evening. Not that I am hiding from anything, or anyone, in particular. I decide it is safer for everyone as well as for my own self-esteem to stay in my room for the rest of the night.

After waking up to pounding and sawing the next day, I begin to sort through boxes and lay some folded clothes in the dresser. Once I was done making some room, I was going to have a burial for my comfort zone sweats. I grab the piece of paper sticking out of the pocket and unfold it. My list. I open it and run through the list of alcohol-induced life expectations for myself. Number one – Make a list. Smart, Sarah. Good one.

I really do need to start making plans though. As much fun as I am having hanging out with Aunt Raines and face-planting into the floor every night, I need to get back on track. I guess I just felt that by sitting around wallowing all day and night meant I was letting them all win. Not that I hoped they thought about me. Well maybe a little. Let's be honest. I was secretly online searching witchcraft spells so I could get into both their inner thoughts until they were sick to death with guilt. Since I haven't heard from either of them, I'm going to assume the website was a hoax. I remind myself to get my money back for that. In the end, I realize I have been sitting around waiting for them to contact me with guilt and complete remorse. I mean, I thought it might take some time, but four months? It may be time to admit that ship has sailed, without me on it. I need to move on.

First thing first, I need to find a job. I just don't know where to look. All the great firms are in the city, and a small part of me fears running into my past there. Knowing it's time I put my big girl pants on, I vow to make today a success. Since I have to start with the basic attire, I search for an outfit. Nothing screams 'I have my shit together so hire me', like Armani slacks and my sheer white Donna Karan blouse. Add a pair of strappy heels, a bit of rouge and some hair primping, and *voila*! We have ourselves a first-class working girl. I look at myself in the mirror and approve. I have to admit, the silk against my skin makes me feel elegant and feminine. It's that or the fact that, for once this week, I actually showered.

I leave my cave and venture downstairs. It is safe to say no one is home. I am also Jack-free since I don't see his truck out front. Not that I'm looking. I grab the newspaper and my laptop and head out, because I have to start somewhere. I don't need a fancy job in a high rise. There are plenty of places for me to find work and be completely satisfied. *This is good*—I mentally coach myself. I smile and pick up my list. I take my pen and cross off number twelve - Be my own therapist. Things are looking up.

I spend the whole morning at the Ma and Pop coffee joint down the street. Not my first pick, but they have free WiFi and it is guaranteed to be free of ex co-worker run-ins. I spend a few hours revamping my resume and then sending it out to local companies.

Sifting through the potential options in the paper that sadly may or may not scream *"my future career"*, I email out a bunch of resumes. Three coffees later, four potential job scores and a positive vibe, I set out to personally drop off some resumes to locals businesses. I figure since they are close, it wouldn't hurt to take a peek into what may be. You can always tell what kind of company you're getting yourself into by the type of people they hire to be the face of said company. But then again, Hamilton Corp had Becky Longhorn, so... Moving on.

Good thing I'm learning that nothing lasts forever, because after entering three offices, it seems the only thing they took from me was my good mood. No resume. No interview. The day is getting late and I am quickly losing my mojo to become employed. I figure if I head home right after my last stop, I can make it in time to meet Aunt Raines in the kitchen for happy hour. But then again, I may want to take the day off from that. My track record after time spent with Aunt Raines has not been looking good for me lately.

I reach my final destination and park the car. Pressing down the growing wrinkles of my pants from the long drive across town, I head towards the office. I turn the corner and realize that the company is based on the upper level lofts, located exactly above one of the newest Macys suburban stand-alone boutiques. I stop for a moment and stare at my past. *Literally*. I stare at the beautiful window display featuring the outside signage and marketing scheme, all perfect and elegant. Just as I had planned it. The last big thing I gave to Hamilton Corp before my blowout was the marketing plan for the new Macys boutiques that were expanding from the Michigan Avenue stores to the nearest southwest suburbs. Now the thought of that day is so dreadful it makes me ill.

I remember stepping out of a two-hour sales pitch and locking down the new Macys boutique proposals. I could feel my body radiating with adrenaline. For weeks I had worked on this project and perfected it exactly to what the clients had been asking for. Their vision in words was my image on paper. No detail missed, and all my bells and whistles attached, I easily landed the signed deal. Shaking hands with the Macys Marketing Board, and walking them out of the office, the restraint not to skip and jump all the way back to my office was strenuous. Things couldn't have gone better. Not to mention the hefty bonus that came along with making Macys extremely happy. I strolled over to Steve's office, which was down the hall, closest to the presidential suites. Being the son of the President gets you a pretty fancy office and view. His secretary stopped me in front of his door.

"I'm sorry Ms. Sullivan, but Steve is out of the office. Is there something I can help you with?"

"Hi Becky. Is Steve in the building or in a meeting?" I hadn't been aware that he had any client meetings offsite that day.

Becky scrambled up the post-it note collection on her desk in a nervous fashion. Unsure what her restlessness was all about, I took a peek into Steve's office and noticed he had not been in at all that day.

"Um yes, I'm sorry, Steve is not in. He has a meeting offsite today. He is not expected in until later. Is there anything you want to leave for him, or a message in case he calls in?"

"No, that's OK. I can call his cell. Everything OK?" I asked.

"Yep, thanks. I'll let him know you came by when he gets in."

"Thanks, do that." I nodded and stepped away, heading back to my office. Not that Becky was ever that cordial but something was up with her today. I brushed her off and went to my office to make celebration plans. This night was going to be huge. First, I made reservations for two at our favorite upscale Fusion Japanese restaurant. This treat was going to be on me due to the extravagant bonus coming my way. Next stop was a department store, because my shoe collection was in major need of a new pair of Manolos, and because nothing says 'congratulations, you're awesome', like Mr. Blahnik.

With the Macys contract signed, I decided to call it a day. I let Jillian, my assistant, know I was leaving for the day and to forward any important calls to my cell. Then I headed out and spent the next two hours adopting the most beautiful new pair of shoes.

Satisfaction couldn't have been any sweeter at that point. The possibilities after this deal were endless. I was in an extra giving mood that day so I also made a pit stop at the lingerie section and picked out a very seductive, very see-through red garment that I knew Steve would definitely approve of. The night was going to be full of celebrations.

I got home right around two in the afternoon, just in time to catch the latest Golden Girls rerun episode. My plan was set into action: a little TV, shower, primp, celebration. I dug my keys out of my purse and unlocked the door. I fumbled with the lock because of all my new bags and finally got the door open. I entered the apartment and moved to drop my bags off on the kitchen island. Then I noticed the pile of mail on the counter and began to sort through—mostly junk.

I paused suddenly as I heard noises coming from the back bedrooms. Knowing I should be alone, my panic began to rise. Who was in the apartment? Stacey should have been at work. Slowly, I dropped my mail and made my way towards the bedrooms. The closer I got, the more animated the sounds became.

Oh my god, I thought, was someone having sex? I passed my bedroom and concluded it was definitely coming from Stacey's room. Wow, I didn't even know she was seeing anyone. Even closer, I saw the door was a bit cracked. I heard the audible sounds of two people definitely in a heated sexual moment.

I actually began to laugh at Stacey's random act. It was definitely not like her to have random men at the apartment in the middle of the day. Feeling a bit guilty but a little intrigued, I continued lurking closer to her door.

The closer I got to the sounds, the less I laughed. The more I heard the sounds of two people, the more I recognized more than just Stacey's. I could feel the color draining from my face. As much as I fought against it, when I got to the door, my arm lifted and pushed the door to its full openness.

The scene before me was like witnessing an accident in slow motion: wishing you could turn away before the final impact, but you just can't force your eyes away from it. In front of me, I watched Steve's naked body slam into Stacey's.

I could do nothing but stare in disbelief at the two most important people in my life, their naked bodies intertwined. I watched as his mouth connected with her chest, while her hands grabbed for his backside. The slapping sounds and curling moans that were echoing from the walls were agonizing.

I fought for air and braced for the door, and my struggle to breathe broke their heavy movements. Both their heads swung in my direction. Steve made eye contact with me first. His facial expression was one for the books. "Shit..." he spat out, winded. He practically threw himself out of— and then off of—Stacey. Landing on two feet and bare naked, he realized his nudity and grabbed at the sheet that Stacey was now grasping for dear life.

"Shit, Shit! Sarah, this is not what it looks like."

My legs were not working with my brain because my brain was telling me to either run or fight, but I did neither. I stood there in complete shock at the view in front of me and prayed it was just a bad dream.

After their little tug-of-war with the sheet, Steve gave up and went in search of his boxers. He stumbled to get them over his two feet and approached me. I felt the ground crumble under me as my knees gave way and I grabbed at the doorframe in an attempt to hold my body up. Steve tried to grab me before I fell. At that moment I lifted my arm and my hand connected with his face. Stunned by my response, he stayed silent.

"What... What is happening here?" I struggled to ask the question I was pretty sure I already knew the answer to. I didn't know how to process what I witnessed, but I knew it was not good. I looked at Stacey. She was sitting in the bed with her 300-thread count Egyptian cotton sheet perfectly wrapped around her. Her face was filled with panic, but she remained speechless. At that moment I felt like I was in a sinking ship of emotions, like the water was sucking me in and the sharp coldness of their betrayal was pulling me under.

"Sarah, this is not what it looks like," Steve said again.

"Oh Steve, stop it. She obviously should know now." Finally Stacey spoke up and her words were like searing knives cutting into my soul.

"I should finally know what?" Finally? *Finally* know? Oh my god. A *finally know* comment translated to *this was not the first time*. Was there something that I had been missing? I grabbed the doorframe again, trying to get a hold of my body and my emotions.

"Stacey, shut up. Listen Sarah. Let's sit down." Steve reached for his pants and tugged them up his legs, then jerked towards me to grab my arms. Stacey slowly made her way out of bed to get her robe.

"This is not happening." I started to shake. As I began to step back, out of the doorframe, Steve caught my arm and grabbed me in a hard grip.

"Stop. This is nothing. Listen to me," Steve responded in an annoyed tone.

I attempted to pull my arms away from his rough grasp but he wouldn't allow it.

"Steve, let go of me! You're hurting me."

"I am not hurting you, I am getting your attention. Now calm down. This can be talked through."

"Steve, let her go, she is fine. She can handle this." Hearing Stacey's voice and the way she spoke to Steve, it was as if they had a plan for this day all along, for when it finally happened.

"Get your hand off of me," I spat out in a strained voice. This was not happening. These two people who I loved were not doing this to me.

Eventually Steve let go, knowing at this point he was probably starting to bruise my arm. I turned around and walked back down the hallway. I heard Stacey and Steve arguing, then two sets of footsteps following me into the living room.

"Now Sarah, listen, this can easily be explained."

I whipped around to face him. "Easily be explained!? What is there to explain!? Are you going to tell me that I saw different from what I did!?"

Steve stepped closer in an attempt to reach me. "You are overreacting. Calm down. This anger does not suit you." I went to swing at him again, but this time he caught my arm. "Like I said, Sar, this anger does not suit you. Now you can calm down and listen or you can act like a child and assume what you want."

He was insane! That was the only conclusion I had come to at that point. I knew Steve was always about being proper and well put together. Image was everything to him. That's exactly why he had molded me into his perfect little arm candy. At this point I believe I was in shock. I tried to catch my breath, but air was not filling my lungs fast enough. I took my eyes off of Steve and re-directed my stare at Stacey. To my disbelief, she looked away from me.

I turned my back to both of them and made it to the kitchen, then I grabbed my purse and fled the apartment. Without having my own transportation, I practically ran four blocks until my heals started to create blisters on my feet and forced me to slow down. It took me seven blocks until I couldn't take it anymore and I broke down and sobbed.

As the memory fades and slowly brings me back to reality, I pull my eyes away from the display. Such a great accomplishment tainted by a horrible realization. I probably didn't even get credit for the end work. I look down at the resume in my hand. During my flashback I managed to crunch the pages, with white knuckles to prove it. The heavy weight of failure feels like sandpaper in my hands. I crunch the paper into a ball and toss it in the public trashcan aligning the street. Always defeated. That's how I feel. Why I thought I was ready to get back on the horse, I'm not sure. That horse kicked me off, remember?

Getting madder with every second that passes by, wondering why I even thought to make this step, I storm to the station wagon and get in. I throw myself into the car and bang my closed fists against the steering wheel. "I hate them for doing this to me," I whisper to myself. I lay my head against the wheel in an effort to regain my composure, then I start the car and set my mental GPS to *Home*, because this job search is officially over. I turn up the radio because I need noise to drown out my aching memories. If my life wasn't already a walking joke, I would have enjoyed a bit more of the humor when Pat Benatar's 'Love is a Battlefield' began blaring though my speakers.

Chapter 11

With my tail between my legs and my mood in the toilet, I make it back home without any accidents. While pulling the big red box into the driveway I notice Jack is sitting in his truck. I look at the time. I would have assumed he'd be done for the day. Being the head honcho of a major construction company, one wouldn't assume the boss stuck around on small job sites. I get out of the car, attempting to do it in a slow sexy way, only to trip over my foot and stumble down into the lawn. *Go figure.* I stand up and pull myself together while Jack jumps out of his truck and heads my way.

"Hey," he calls out, walking up the driveway. God, why does his simple 'Hey' sound so seductive, like *'Hey. Let's get naked'*?

 "Hey yourself," I repeat. How more lame can I sound?!

He makes his way to the side of the Stabbin Wagon. "You OK?"

"Oh yeah, I dropped an earring in the lawn. Was just picking it up."

He looks at me and says, "So the other day. We never got to finish our adventure of replacing that top of the line smartphone that somehow bit it into traffic.

"Oh yeah. That. No problem. Seems that the world minus technology is actually working out for me," I say.

We stand there eye-locked for what seems like eternity. His *sex me* eyes have me in a trance, and my ability to conjure up a sentence fails me. "You still with me?" *Huh?*

"Huh? Yeah. So don't worry about it. Phones are extremely overrated. I'm going to start a trend. No phones. Live free!" *Shut up, Sarah.*

Jack chuckles. "Well, then let me make it up to you at least in the form of dinner and drinks?" I'm pretty sure I'm just staring at him again since he has rendered me speechless. *Did he just ask me out?*

"Did you just ask me out?"

More chuckling. "Well, I guess you can call it that," he says. "Unless you have other plans. You do seem to be setting a record with how much vermouth one can indulge in." My cheeks turn red faster than humanly possible. He steps closer to me, closing in the space between us. "I didn't mean to embarrass you. I just meant that I found it quite impressive. And if you wouldn't mind, over some food and drinks, you can teach me your secret." At this, I laugh. "Nice save?" he asks.

"Nice save," I tell him. "You look like a good student. I will accept your offer. And teach you all my ways." I notice his body relax as I accept. He returns my answer with a breathtaking smile.

"Great. I'll pick you around seven?" He wears a smile that might actually resemble satisfaction.

"Yep. I'll see you at seven." I then side-step out of his line of vision, because at this point he almost has me pinned to the car, and I'm about ready to move up our plans and invite him to the backseat of the Shaggin' Wagon. I give him a warm smile and head up to the door. Before I hit the stoop, he calls out my name.

"Sarah?"

"Yeah?" I respond and turn around.

"Try and stay clear of your Aunt Raines," he says with a hint of humor in his voice.

Man, he's good. I give him the head-nod in acknowledgment and turn to walk inside. I can hear Aunt Raines in the kitchen shaking up her daily concoction. I bee-line it straight upstairs.

Chapter 12

I hit my bedroom and slip inside unnoticed. I would really hate to have to turn down poor Aunt Raines, because it's just simply wrong to drink alone. But I also need to focus. It's starting to set in that I was just asked out. By Jack. As in get dressed up and go out, and do what people do on dates.

What do people do on dates!? Panic completely starts to set in! I can't remember the last time I was on a date. I start pulling open boxes in search of my clothes. I should have labeled these boxes with 'I have given up' which you will find my shirts and sweats in, and 'I will eventually be on a date, and I need to look hot'. I settle with just knocking over all of the boxes until I rip open one and pull out my dresses. I pick out a nice red low-cut, strappy-shoulder dress that stops just above my knees. I hang it up and match a stellar pair of gold Prada stilettos.

I jump in the shower to do a good scrub-down. One can never be too sure where an innocent date can lead to, and knowing me I wouldn't mind if our date consisted of just the inside of his truck. Pushing aside my dirty thoughts, I scrub, shave, exfoliate and get out. Blow dry my hair, check. Lotion, check. Makeup, simple and...check. I grab my dress and shuffle it over my head. As I slip my second shoe on my foot, I stand up straight and give myself a good look over.

Shockingly, my response at my finished product is not what I expected. I look at myself in my dress with my made-up hair and my simple features. I look exactly like the person that Steve would approve of. This isn't me. This was him. The person he, over the years, molded me into.

Before I met Steve, I hated dresses. It was at the hands of Stacey's money and Steve's influence that my wardrobe became more sophisticated. Not to brag, but I have great hair. It is full and vibrant (when I kept up color of course), but Steve always insisted I kept it up and neat. Red was Steve's favorite color so I spent most of my paychecks searching for red attire, hoping he would notice and approve. I don't even like the color red. This isn't me!

So disgusted at who I see, I rip my hair down, hearing the pins scatter on the floor. I step out of my shoes and tear off my dress. Having a bit of a break-down after the zipper gets stuck, I literally tear it off. Hearing the dress rip down the back, I throw my body out of it and toss it violently into the trash. I start to breathe heavily and know I am just milliseconds away from having a complete meltdown.

"Why are they still doing this to me?" I whisper sadly to myself. They aren't even here and they are still pulling me down. Thinking they are probably at some ritzy restaurant right now having a fancy meal with one another while sharing a good laugh at my expense, I slide down to the floor and lay my face in my hands. This has to stop soon, right?

"Sarah?" I hear my mom call through the door. "Jack is downstairs waiting. Are you coming down, honey?"

"I'll be right down, Mom!" I say, trying to hide the strain in my voice. I stand up and try to get my emotions in check. I think for a second to tell my mom that I have suddenly gotten ill and to please tell Jack we have to reschedule, but I know he would just think I was weak and took a detour to the kitchen to visit with Aunt Raines when I came in.

I set my shoulders straight and look in the mirror. "You can do this. You are hot. You are funny. You are a good person, and you deserve this." I repeat this little mantra to myself twice over until I feel some confidence return. I try to remember what I was like before Shitstorm Steve hit; I was carefree and wild. I need to find that girl again and things will be OK. I reach for my brush and let my hair fully down. I dig into my makeup case and give myself some hot smoky eyes and dab my lips with gloss. I run back into my room and find my tight skinny jeans and green halter top, which pretty much screams 'I have a fabulous rack, would you like to see?' I keep the gold stilettos because I love them and they never did anything wrong to me, so they stay. Lastly, I spritz a bit of perfume and exit my bedroom.

Chapter 13

I walk down the stairs and can hear my mom talking with Jack about the progress of the addition. I hear her praising him for the work his men have accomplished. I didn't think he would produce anything less. He seems so dedicated to his work, and so detailed. His hard work and confidence radiated off him when he spoke to clients and directed his crew. Any person would be proud of him.

Hitting the last step, I stop to admire the view and take a good look at him. His presence sends warm chills down my lady parts. He has changed into a button-up charcoal shirt and a new pair of jeans. His black blazer hangs just right on his broad shoulders. His dark hair, still damp from a shower, is combed back in a messy wave.

I can tell my mom hears my arrival because she wraps up her praises and excuses herself into the kitchen. I hit the bottom step and see Jack turn his attention to me. Our eyes connect and for a moment he just stares at me.

"Everything OK?" I ask, nervous that I might have toilet paper stuck to my face or something.

"Wow," he says, still staring.

"Is my shirt inside out?" I instinctively look down, feeling my shirt for outside seams.

"No, no. You just look...stunning."

He starts to walk towards me. As I step down the last stair to walk his direction, he stops in front of me. "I'm sorry." He pauses. "I just wasn't expecting... Wow." He looks at me in bewilderment. The warmth and satisfaction I feel at the way he is looking at me is so fulfilling, knowing I am finally showing the real me.

"Apparently I need to clean up more often around you then," I say to break the ice.

Jack wraps his hand around my waist and bends his head down to my ear. "I would have taken you either way," he whispers. Then he pulls away, now rendering me speechless, and begins to lead me towards the door. I think I say goodbye to my mom, but I'm not sure. I might have actually floated out of the house with him, to his truck.

Chapter 14

After Jack helps me into his manly macho truck, we head to the next town over while we discuss our evening plans. He insists on taking us to a nice restaurant, but I insist we not. We settle on a tavern in mid-town that has great pool, all the beers on tap you can think of, and an even better bar food menu.

We are seated at a table closer to the back, by a waitress who seriously needs to get her manners in check. Ogling at my date the whole way to our seat is not getting her any brownie points with me. Note to self: Skimp on her tip.

Not even noticing the Skanktress, Jack pulls out my chair for me to sit. "What can I get you to drink?" the McSkanktress asks, looking only in Jack's direction.

"Whatever she wants and then I'll have the same," Jack says, looking at me with a devilish grin. So maybe he is not completely blind to this skanky waitress's antics. Good boy.

After making her recite every single beer on tap, which was about 21, then asking her to repeat them all, due to my poor memory of course, I order us two Belgian brewed taps and send her on her skanky way.

"Bad memory huh?" He laughs, settling in his chair.

"That will teach her to work a little less hard for her tips," I tell him, and we start laughing, both witnessing the scowl on her face as she stands by the bar reciting our order.

"So..." I begin. "How did you or your dad get into the construction business?"

"Well, my dad inherited the business from his dad. Started out small and local. Would do just small jobs for locals, neighbors, you know. Then my dad turned a few jobs into a lot of jobs, and saved every penny to begin his own separate company building houses and taking on bigger jobs here and there. I would work for him during the summers when I was home from school. Then the summer after I graduated college, he had a heart attack while driving to a site, and died. Left me everything. I couldn't let all his years of hard work die with him, so I basically picked up where he left off."

Wow. I was not expecting it to get so deep, so fast. It makes me feel sorry for Jack, losing a parent. It makes me want to comfort him for his loss and his sacrifice. "I'm sorry again to hear about your dad."

"Don't be, it was a long time ago. He was a great man."

I try moving us along to lighter topics. "You said after college... What did you get your degree in?"

"I graduated from MIT with a degree in Architecture," he answers back with a nonchalance in his voice, but I can sense a bit of regret in his tone.

Our bar maid at this moment decides to return with our drinks. She hands Jack his first of course then puts mine by me without even looking my way. "Is there anything else you need right now?" she asks, practically batting her eyes him. Is this chick for real?

"Nope, I have everything I want right in front of me," he responds without taking his eyes off of me. The Bar Hooch clicks her tongue in annoyance and turns her tail back to the bar. I think I'm in love with this man.

We spend the next two hours talking and getting to know each other. Jack is simply amazing. I learn that he and I share the same interest in basically everything. I also learn sadly that after college he had landed a major spot in a huge architecture firm but had to walk away from it when his dad died. He told me he lived just across town in a small ranch that he and his dad built. He said it was still a work in progress, and he was only able to work on it when business was slow, which wasn't too often the last couple of years. I told him about my reckless college bar stories and what I thought I might want to do with my life, though I wasn't quite so sure anymore. He asked about Aunt Raines, and I gave him the full story, happiness, Uncle Merle and all.

Three games of pool, a few lagers and a really grouchy waitress later, I am feeling really relaxed and carefree. "You up for one more game of pool, or are you done having me whoop your ass?" he says.

I giggle at his comment, because it's the truth. He washed me of three straight games. At this point I'm not only feeling carefree, but I'm also feeling a little bold. That's what international lager will do to you. "Oh, you betcha."

Jack laughs. "Good. I'm going to run to the bathroom real quick. Get the table ready for your last and final defeat." At that I stick my tongue out at him. Because it's mature and I'm well on my way to being a bit drunk. I watch Jack walk away and fail to take my eyes away from his swaying ass. What I wouldn't do to wrap my hands around those tight cheeks and squeeze, while under... *Geez, get your head out of the gutter, Sarah.* I turn to the table and begin to gather the balls.

"Hey Sweetheart, you look like you can use a friend." Startled, as hands wrap around my waist, I whip around to face a dude I do not recognize with a smirk on his face.

"Get your hands off me," I say a bit nervous, because this guy is huge and doesn't look like he knows the word no.

"Why don't you and I have a dance or two and get to know each other better?"

Debating how fast I can take my pool stick and bash it across this guy's face and run, I thankfully sense Jack as he steps possessively behind me. "You need something, buddy?"

"Yeah," he says. "Looks like this little lady needs some company and you seemed to have left so I'm steppin in."

"Are you kidding me, pal?" Jack spits out. There it is. That anger. The same anger he directed at me the first day I met him on the street. Being on the other end of his anger now, I can't help but feel completely turned on by his dominance. Jack grabs at my hand in an attempt to guide me behind him, most likely in case fists are to be thrown down.

"I ain't kiddin' man, you wanna go?" the creepy dude asks. "I'll take you out for a piece of that ass."

Just then, Jack lunges at the guy. Taking his fist swiftly to the guy's nose, I watch as the guy's head jerks back and slams against the wall. "You want more, pal? Or did you want me to explain to you a little bit more that she is taken, and it ain't by you."

"Fuck you, man! You just broke my nose!"

Jack goes to strike again, when another guy approaches in an attempt to break things up. "Dale, it's OK man, let it go. Let's get out of here."

"Yeah *Dale*," Jack says. "I think it's time you get the fuck outta here. "

The guy spits out blood that is dripping from his nose.

"Fuck you and your fucking whore."

Before Jack can lunge again I step in front of him and place both of my hands on his chest. The guy's buddy drags the other guy away, out of the bar, and leaves us standing by the pool table. Jack is breathing heavily. If I'm not mistaken, he seems to be shaking. He takes both of his hands and swipes his fingers through his hair, then he steps out of my reach and goes to sit back at the table. I stand there, debating on when it is a good time to intercept his mood. I walk slowly back to the table and sit down in my seat across from him.

"Hey, you OK?" I ask. He doesn't respond. "You wanna talk about what just happened?"

"I'm sorry," he says. "If I ruined the night and you want me to take you home, that's fine—"

"No, it's cool," I say. "I love when men get all caveman on me. I just wanted to make sure you're OK. You got pretty angry back there."

"I'm sorry. As you have witnessed enough by now, I have a bit of a temper. I guess I am no better than you with my experiences with people who can't keep their hands to themselves. I don't want to get into it, but obviously there's an ex..." Jack takes a deep breath to calm himself down, but I can tell he's still in his head while he tries to finish with his explanation. I feel the need to shift the mood immediately, because this sore topic is not one that either of us wants to dwell on, I'm sure.

Since I have had a lot to drink tonight, I think to do the only thing I know will calm Jack down completely, and the only thing I know I've been aching to do since we got to the bar.

I stand up, failing miserably in my attempt not to stumble, and walk around the table to Jack's chair. He slowly turns so his legs are now out from under the table, and I step in closer to place my hips in-between his thighs. I raise my hands and wrap my arms around his neck.

Jack stares at me, his eyes glazed over with desire. Obviously fighting back the urge to take over, he allows me to follow through with my mission. Once I get a good grasp around his neck, I lock eyes with him. *God, he is beautiful.*

Slowly, I lower my head and press my lips against his. His mouth is warm and inviting. I'm pretty sure we both feel the spark that shoots through us once our lips touch, and our tongues connect. Just then, he decides he can't stand back any longer and takes control, deepening our kiss.

Jack raises his hands and wraps his strong warm arms around my waist, tugging me closer in-between his thighs and against his chest. I just can't get enough of this man. I tighten my hold on his neck even harder and press my body into his. I can feel the massive delight straining his jeans. Our tongues connect for round two and that erotic spark goes off again. I'm pretty sure a moan just uncurled from the back of my throat and escaped my mouth.

This might be the hottest thing that I have ever done. Openly making out in a bar with a gorgeous guy! I mean, I am participating in PDA and it is so hot. My inner self takes a spin and bows. Just as...

"Sarah?" I hear from behind me.

I break away from Jack's mouth and gasp for air. With him still holding me close, I turn around.

...Stacey

What the hell is she doing here? I look past her to see a private table, with a group of clients—by the looks of them. I forget not everyone is unemployed. I turn my eyes back to Stacey. She stands looking at me a few feet from our table, holding the Gucci clutch purse that hangs from around her shoulder. Her shiny hair is in a perfect ponytail, and she's dressed in what is most likely an Armani skirt and blouse. Looking not a stitch out of place, she radiates as if life has been nothing but great for her. I feel my body stiffen in Jack's arms.

"I'm sorry to interrupt," she says. "I saw you just as I was on my way out. I was going to leave but I wanted to see if maybe, hopefully, we could talk."

This is not happening. She has to be kidding me right now! I am literally speechless. Four months away from them, away from that job, that life, and I come face-to-face with Stacey in some random bar while on my first date with Jack. I assume Jack can feel me start to shake because he suddenly holds me tighter.

I dreamt about this moment for months. The things I would say if put in front of her. I would ask her how she could have done that to me. Years and years of friendship, worth nothing because she chose to throw it all away. Now that it's happening, I don't even know where to start, what to do. I just freeze.

"Sarah, are you going to say anything? I'm sorry, please talk to me. You don't understand. I miss you! I messed up, I'm so sorry..." Then she begins to softly cry. Waiting for me to say anything at all, she continues. "You just left, and didn't give me an opportunity to explain. Steve lied to me too. He made all these promises to me and—"

That. Is. It.

The only instinct that kicks in is my arm movement. I raise my hand and smack her across the face. The sound echoes across the bar. People turn and on-lookers stop playing their games and turn toward us. Stacey grabs her face while staring at me in complete shock.

I watch Stacey's mouth gape open at the realization of my actions, and she steps towards me. "How dare you! You ungrateful—" she begins, and I go to raise my hand again for round two. That's when Jack stands up, grabs my arm and braces my body against his. I fight against his hold to get at her because I am going to claw her goddamned eyes out!

While trying to maneuver my whaling body, Jack flips a bunch of bills on the table, then throws me over his shoulder and starts walking out of the bar. Before getting to the door, I lift up my head to stare Stacey down. Facing our way, she is still staring at us, her open mouth gaping like a fish out of water.

"I feel sorry for you, Stacey. You can have him!" I spit out, right before we step out of the door.

Jack carries me until we are just outside his truck. He slowly sets me down and holds both hands around my shoulders to assess my mood. He's probably debating if he should let go or not, whether I am going to bolt and go back inside the bar for a final blow.

"Are you OK?" he asks, measuring my mood.

"I'm great," I say. "Couldn't be better." Lie.

If I let you go are you going to start running?"

"No." Lie. Lie.

"Are you lying to me?"

"No." Lie. Lie. Lie. Man, he is like all in my head right now?

I can't seem to catch my breath. I feel my fight dying off and giving in to the sadness and regret that I feel. Then my shoulders slump on Jack's hands and I lay me head on his chest. I begin to cry, because I really don't know how else to express my overwhelming emotions right now.

Jack adjusts his arms and moves his hands from my shoulders so they are now wrapped around me. Beyond my soft cries, I can hear him telling me it's OK. I knew this day would come, I just didn't know how hard it was going to be. To look Stacey in the face and hope to see the guilt wash over her features. The shame and the admittance of what she did to me. All which after seeing did nothing to erase what happened. The worst part of it was that she thought she could just come to me and apologize and as always I would be the pushover and accept. Brush it under the table and we can go on being who we were. It makes me sick to think how fake our friendship actually was.

I gradually pull myself together, and stop crying. I look up at Jack and his eyes are so soft and understanding. He helps me in the truck and shuts my door for me. Seconds later, he climbs in the driver's side and starts the car.

"I'm sorry…" I say while looking away from him.

"Don't be. Do you want to talk about it?"

"Not sure there is anything else to add in. I'm sure you got the gist from good ole' Becky the other day. I met Stacey and Steve pretty much right out of college. Stacey was my roommate and best friend. Steve was my boyfriend for seven years. We worked together. The corporation I worked for was actually owned by his father. We were together for close to seven years. Now that I look back, I'm not sure how many of those years we were actually exclusive. I came home one day to find Stacey and Steve in bed together, in the nice apartment I shared with Stacey. Neither one attempted to save grace. They let me leave. I showed up at work a few days later, and went bonkers on Steve in front of the entire board. Threw a few harsh words around, vocally gave my resignation, and walked out. Then I paid a service to pack my things out of the apartment, and ended up on my parents' doorstep a little while later. Go figure. The one place I was so eager to get away from."

Jack doesn't say anything back. He just listens. At some point in my explanation he had taken my hand in his.

"I'm sorry that happened to you."

"Don't be, please. I don't need anyone's pity," I say, then I snatch my hand away from his. That was not the response I was looking for.

"I didn't say it to feel sorry for you, Sarah. I said it because I'm sorry you had to go through that. I'm *not* sorry you are not with someone anymore that could have just thrown something like you away." When he finishes, he grabs my hand and places it back in his. Then he pulls our joined hands to his lips and presses a gentle kiss to the back of my palm. He looks me in the eyes and squeezes my hand.

We are silent for some time before I break the ice again.

"I'm sorry, Jack. It's just hard to have people look at me as the pathetic one who had to crawl back home. I have spent too much time over the past months feeling sorry for myself that I just can't have someone else joining in on the pity party."

"Then stop letting it," he says.

"Excuse me?"

"Stop feeling sorry or pity for yourself. You didn't do anything wrong, Sarah. You were sideswiped by two individuals that didn't think past themselves. I've known you less than two weeks and all I can focus on is your charm and humor. You're beautiful and smart. Your ambition and success is all because you pushed yourself and you got there. I see nothing but amazing. You should too. If they didn't, then screw 'em."

I stare at him. Simply stare.

"Thank you," I whisper.

Jack lets out a soft chuckle. "You don't need to thank me either, Sarah. I'm just telling you what I see."

I am not sure anyone in my entire life has said something so kind and so genuine. I think I definitely love him. And every time my name leaves his tongue it sends a jolting spark straight down my stomach, right to my golden spot.

Jack finally pulls into my driveway and sets the truck in park. He adjusts his body so he is slanted in my direction and starts to speak. Like a wild tiger, I jump over the seat and throw myself onto his lap. I crush my lips to his and nonverbally thank him for his kind words. He responds instantly and grabs my hips and crushes my body to his. I can't get enough of his mouth. He tastes so good. I feel like I say that a lot.

"I can't get enough of your mouth," I mutter between tongue lashes, not certain it sounds like more than a muffle.

"You taste so good," he responds while adjusting my mouth to kiss me deeper.

"It's probably the aftertaste of the hops. *No one* can resist a good lager," I say breathlessly then reconnect with his mouth.

He pulls away just a hair to speak. "No, it's you. You taste fantastic. The smell of your skin. The feel of your tongue.

I'm not sure I'm going to be able to stop kissing you this time."

My heart abruptly stops. I pull away and stare into his beautiful eyes. At this point they are blaring black orbs, screaming desire for me.

Jack takes his hands and puts pressure against the back of my head to bring me closer to his mouth. "I thought I just told you I didn't want this kiss to stop?" he says in a bit of frustration and teasing tone.

"I don't know where you came from, but thank you," I tell him quickly and place my lips back where they belong. He opens my mouth with his tongue and we reconnect with a spark that sends both of us moaning. He slides one hand down my back and connects with my butt, then lightly squeezes. This may be the hottest thing I have done ever. I thought the bar scene was hot, but this might be topping it. I am straddling this hunk of a man in his macho truck, while he does his magic to my mouth and my body.

My head is swimming, I am so lost in emotion. My body is screaming to be ravished right in this truck. My heart is aching to just hold on and my brain is, well, mush at this point. I am like a wound-up alley cat in heat, ready to explode. Anxiously, I push back from him and send my shaky hands straight to his pants. I make a weak attempt to unbutton his pants, while his free hand moves to the front of my stomach and inside my shirt. *Oh, heavens above*. His hands are so hot on my skin, I'm sure that he is going to leave marks. While he moves upward towards my Bs, I push my butt back to get better access. If I don't touch goods in less than five seconds, I'm going to cry. I jerk my butt back further which lands on the steering wheel, sending the horn honking dramatically into the night. We break apart, startled by the unwanted sound. We are both breathing heavily and are struggling to get our crazed emotions in order. We take the next couple of seconds to stare at each other before I break the silence.

"Holy cow," I whisper very slowly.

Jack's only response is a soft chuckle. He takes his hand from under my shirt and presses the lever on the side to adjust the seat back.

Then, in the distance, we notice the front porch light turn on. Probably my mom wondering why there's a blaring horn going off outside the window. I take one last look at Jack and separate my lower self from his lap. I may have groaned out loud at the loss of his warm body. We both sit in his truck staring forward for a minute until the light goes off.

"Well," I say." I'm not sure where that came from, but thank you."

Jack laughs again. "Well, you're welcome, and come back soon."

I giggle in return. We fall silent again.

"I should go inside. My mother is probably sitting there peeking out the blinds, waiting to catch me in action. Unfortunately I lacked adolescent outbursts when I was younger. This might be making up for all the lost years of catching her teenage daughter in the act."

"Sure."

"Thanks for the wonderful, albeit eventful, evening. I'll...uh...I'll see you around," I say, pretty sure with a teenage blush in my cheeks.

Jack nods at me in amusement.

Seeing as it's my cue to exit stage left, I open the door and jump out. I walk to the front door and look back at Jack who is still staring my way. I give him the lame-o wave, because at this point my brain has taken a sabbatical, and walk inside.

I shut the door behind me and lean against the wooden frame. I stand there until I can no longer hear the purrs of his truck engine. After what feels like ages, I take in a huge breath and exhale. The light in the living room suddenly shoots on, and I jump up probably three feet in the air. I see my mother crouched over by the couch in a lean-to position.

"Oh boy, does that man look like a nice kisser..."

I gape at my mother in horror. "What?! You scared the hell out of me!"

"Well that would seem to happen, when your head is stuck in the gutter, dear," she says, and then she climbs off the couch, walks past me, and up the stairs back to bed.

Mental reminder: Move out of my parents' house.

Chapter 15

I love dreaming. I was always one who could dream all night and be able to remember them when I woke up. Depending on what was going on in my life, the food I ate, the drinks I consumed, my dreams were always so wild and out there. They always felt so real. At my current state of dreaming, I am in the most wondrous position you can think of. Lying on my back, I have Jack on top on me, and my legs are wrapped around his strong waist. My hands are working their way down his bare chest. The touch of his hard body sends a wave of ecstasy down my spine.

I work my hands down past his hard abs and make my way to his backside to grab his firm ass. Oh god, he is so hard and delicious, and oh god, I can feel his bulge press against my lady parts as his head dips into the curve of my neck and he begins to nibble his way up to my ear. *Oh god, I love dreams*. I can hear his voice calling my name and it's about the one thing that is going to send me over the edge.

"Sarah?" I hear it again, and holy mother is his voice so real and hot against my ear, moving his way around my neck.

"Oh Jack..." I whimper, possibly out loud since this is getting way too intense.

His hands feel so real, grazing against my cheek. "Yes?"

What the hell?

My eyes fly open to a very close, real-life Jack leaning over me with a guilty twinkle in his eyes. My reaction is swift and not smooth, as I fly up head-first straight forward, making contact with his head. We both touch our heads.

"Ouch!" he says. "Why did you just head butt me?"

"What are you doing in here?" I say quite frantically, rubbing at my forehead. How long has he been in here? Oh god, was I just moaning his name?

"Well, you were moaning my name," he echoes.

Kill. Me. Now.

"What are you doing in my room?" I sit up, pulling my blankets closer to my chest.

"Your mother let me in. Her and your father went for breakfast. Wanted me to let them know when you got up. But I see that you were busy enjoying yourself."

Has anyone ever actually died of embarrassment? Because I think I'm about to be the first.

"I'm not really sure what you heard or think what was going on, but I was just having the most horrible dream." Yep, I'm going to try and play this one off.

Jack bursts out laughing.

Fail.

Moving on. "So why are you up here, Jack?" I attempt to regroup the conversation.

"Well I was thinking about your list. And I wanted to make you an offer." He sits down on my bed and adjusts his waist to face me. "Now hear me out before you jump the gun and say no..."

"OK, do I want to know where you're going with this?"

He grabs one of my hands that's clutching the blanket and pulls it down and squeezes. "So," he begins, "I think I have some ideas to help you conquer some of your list. Starting with: Complete a goal. Now here me out. I have some small projects that have been sitting on the backburner at the site. They could use some of your eyes and expertise. I was hoping that in-between job and soul searching, you could spend some time helping me with these projects. I will pay you of course. And I will also make sure you don't stop until they are complete. We both win. I get work that's been building up completed and you cross completing a goal off your list."

He pauses and waits for my reaction. He wants me to work with him? Thinking about getting to spend more time with him on a daily basis is almost a no-brainer right there. But the thought that he actually spent time thinking about how to help me is so touching I don't even know what to say. I want to play it cool, but I doubt I'm able to hide the emotion in my face when I respond.

"Wow, Jack. I think that's really thoughtful that you think I can be of use to you. I would love to help you out…and help cross off a goal of course." I finish speaking quickly. I don't want to look too desperate.

"I have some work to explain to the guys outside then, and if you're up for it, we can take a trip to my site office and I can go over the projects I have, and you can tell me which ones you're interested in."

I'm interested in you. "That would be great."

Jack gets up and leaves me to my thoughts. I hear the kitchen door open and close. *Holy cow!* This guy has to be fake. I get to spend all my day working side-by-side with him and his sexy man self. Oh man! Today is definitely a shower day. I jump out of bed because I have Ke$ha blaring in my head and I'm getting pumped up for this. I begin to dance like a crazy teenager in my room.

I can't remember the last time I felt honest-to-god happy. Ever since Jack came into my life, I feel like I have been able to actually breathe again. And now he is giving me a chance to spread my wings and build my confidence back up. Not that he even explained what I would be doing but that will be another topic of conversation. I simply dance and giggle. I shake my behind and do a little boogie up and down—while spinning of course. Today is going to be an awesome day!

Dance time makes a quick halt because I'm nearly spun-out and about to go down. I start to slow myself down and take a peek out my window, hoping to get a nice look at Jack. To my horrification, he and three foremen are standing there staring up at my window. Shit eatin' grins on their faces as they witness my dance-off.

Mental note #827: I need to get some blinds.

Chapter 16

Shower, check, makeup, check. Tight jeans and semi-showing cleavage shirt, check.

Practically skipping down the steps, I meet Jack outside. He seems to be working with one of his men and directing him to what looks like some of the final stages of the addition. A bit of sadness sets in knowing he will be done with the project at some point and won't be popping up around here every morning.

As I wait for him I think about how good it's going to feel to get back on the horse. Just getting my hands wet with a new project puts a perk back in my step. As much as I now hate anything Hamilton Corp, I still miss the job. I definitely don't miss my last encounter with my co-workers though. For a moment, I lose myself to thoughts of the last day I walked through those doors.

I can't say I am very proud of my actions that day at Hamilton Corp, but as they say, you can't turn back time, so... After running out of the apartment and then breaking down in the middle of an intersection, thankfully a complete stranger saw pity on me and helped me at least get onto a sidewalk. I think the poor woman thought someone had died because who would act like such a fool for anything less than death? Little did she know it was the death of my bubble... Eventually I pulled myself together and made it to a local hotel. I couldn't go back to the apartment and I definitely could not go home.

I'm not sure how, but I made it to a hotel room just in time for my second breakdown. I undressed and threw myself in the shower with the water scolding hot. I cried for how long, I wouldn't even know. The time I spent in the hotel is still a bit blurry to me. I guess when your mind wants to help your heart it causes you to forget, pushing away all the bad. I do know that I eventually crawled out of the shower and into the bed where I slept and cried for two days straight.

It took me that long to stop being so hurt and to begin feeling angry. I remember the heat fueling through my body as I paced the room thinking about what I saw and why. I had given everything to him. I stood by him through all those unspoken moments when he lost his cool and his hands did the talking for him. I played the pretty, perfect girlfriend and did everything for him. I loved him. I couldn't process my questions quickly enough before the next one popped in my head. How long had it been going on? When did it start? Was this the first time? Were they ever going to tell me? Does he even love me? Did he ever love me? But the one major question that kept resurfacing was: how can he do this to me?

Only having the clothes I came in, I threw the hotel robe to the ground and dressed. Not putting any thought to the consequences but only focusing on my anger, I called down to the front desk and checked out. I grabbed my things and hailed a cab, heading straight to Hamilton Corp.

When I got to the 15th floor, the elevator dinged opened and I stormed through. I felt the thick silence in the air as I walked through the building, heading straight towards Steve's office. Right before I hit his door, my eyes caught the conference room door open and a group walking out. Among them was Steve.

It took him a few seconds, which seemed like hours, to catch my scolding stare, and he stopped in his tracks. I could tell he saw the instability in my eyes and that this scene was not going to be as quiet as he hoped.

"Sar..." he said slowly, like trying to calm me down by his slow draw-out of my name.

"When were you going to tell me?" I asked in a calm but threatening tone that sent all eyes around us back and forth from me to Steve.

"Sar, why don't you come into my office and we can talk?"

"I asked you a question, or can you not be honest with that either?! When. Did. YOU start sleeping with my roommate!?"

I could hear the gasps around the entire floor. If I had been more tactful with my breakdown, I probably wouldn't have wished that the entire office had just been informed of Steve's infidelity and my pathetic confrontation.

"Sarah. Quiet down. Now is not the time. I said let's go talk—"

He got mid-way through his sentence when my brain shut off and my impulsiveness took over, and I turned to my left, picked up a plant from his secretary's desk and hurled it towards his head—unfortunately missing him, two board members and his secretary, and it crashed into the conference room wall instead, spraying plant and dirt everywhere.

"I don't need to step into your office, Steve! I need you to fuck off! I hope it was all worth it. Hopefully she can meet your demanding expectations as your pushover arm candy. You and this whole place can shove it! I'm done!

With you! With this place! All of it! I quit! Take *that* to your office!"

I then proceeded to pivot, brush my hands down my skirt to smooth away the fake creases, and walk confidently to the elevator. I pressed the down button and waited while feeling an office full of open-mouthed stares on my back. The door opened and I walked in, hoping the world would swallow me and make me disappear.

"You ready?" Jack catches my attention and breaks my thoughts back to the present. I brush off the negative memories and continue towards his truck. Nothing is going to ruin this new adventure for me.

"Yep," I say. "Let's go, boss," I joke with a warm grin on my face. He walks behind me and gives me a quick spanking on my behind. I jolt at the connection of his hand to my butt. He passes me with a devilish grin on his face, then takes a big leap into the truck.

"So, we have about twenty minutes until we get to my office. Let's use this time to conduct an official interview," he says with humor in his voice. I look over at him and simply laugh.

"Well I would most definitely agree. I mean, I hope you don't just go around hiring anybody," I reply playfully.

"OK, so why don't you tell me what your strengths are?"

I scoot up straighter in my seat and turn to him with a serious look on my face. "Well, Jack. May I call you Jack?" He laughs and nods for me to continue. "Well, I have my degree in Marketing, Jack. I worked at a marketing firm for many years, which qualifies me to basically work magic and solve world hunger. My best ideas come to me when I am being fed gallons of coffee and sugar. Speaking of which, may I ask what sort of caffeine device you have in your office?"

"Oh, well, I believe it is a standard coffee maker. Most definitely not made in this century. Is that going to be a deal breaker for you?"

"We are still in negotiations, Jack. An updated version may need to be my added incentive."

Jack throws his head back and laughs. If I had my phone, I would most likely be recording that sound to listen to later. Or every night before bed. Or during my...*alone time*.

OK, enough Sarah.

Twenty minutes later, we reach Calloway Construction. We both get out of the truck to see all the commotion going on around his site. Jack seems at ease with all the comings and goings of men and materials.

"Wow, this place is busy. Don't you have to be here instructing everyone?" He seems so important. In a way I feel a bit guilty that I am pulling him away from his main focus.

"Everything that runs on this site is supervised by my Site Manager." Jack points to a tall bronzed blond. The guy tips his hard hat, and I recognize him from the other week.

"Ah, McHottie," I say as if in no introductions are even needed.

"Excuse me?" he asks in confusion.

"Oh nothing, we met that one day I came and gave you a run for your money."

Jack laughs and presses his hand on my lower back to signal me to continue walking. We head into the trailer I entered last week and walk back to his office. He opens the door for me and I walk in first. I didn't take the time before to look around, but now that I'm not in such a hurry I take the time to absorb all the framed work and blueprints on the walls.

"Wow, are all these projects you've done?" I ask. They are breathtaking. I can tell they were drawn by someone with a very strong architecture background. They are simply flawless.

Jack walks up to stand next to me while I admire a drawing of a beautiful ranch house looking out on a plot of land. The detail is incredible. "This is my house. My dad and I started working on it together. Once he passed I was only able to work on it here and there. It's done enough for me to live comfortably in it. But it still needs a lot of work."

"Wow," I say as I stare at the drawings and the actual photo prints that are framed alongside it.

"Well, maybe I will have to show you the real thing sometime. I have done amazing things to the bedroom," he adds, looking at me with his cute little sideways grin. When I turn to look at him, I notice a ping of challenge seeping out of his glare.

"Well let me be the judge of that, Mr. Callaway."

It takes two seconds.

Two seconds for him to pin me to the wall and crush his mouth to mine. I can't get his mouth around mine fast enough. Our tongues are lashing into each other's mouths and both sets of hands go into each other's shirts. His hands grab my boobs and we both moan in unison. Oh god, this feels so good. He feels so good. My body fits so perfectly into his embrace. This man might ruin me for any other man. Why am I thinking about any other man right now? God, I just want it to be Jack. I can feel how this is affecting him by the strong bulge in his pants pressing against my stomach. I'm pretty sure the only way this make-out session should end is with us on the floor with our clothes off...

A knock at the door startles us both and Jack pulls away faster than he had attacked. The door opens and McHottie walks through the door frame.

"Hey boss, I needed you to sign—" He looks my way and then at Jack. "Sorry, I didn't know you were preoccupied. I'll come back later," he announces with a suspicious grin that starts to spread along his face. He turns to exit the office.

"Wait, Bill. Just, um. I was just showing Sarah around. Sarah, this is Bill, my Site Manager. She is going to be doing some contracting work for us," Jack explains and gestures his hand towards Bill as an introduction.

"I believe we have already met," Bill says with a glimmer of mischief on his face. Then he steps forward to shake my hand.

"Yes I believe we have. If I remember correctly, you have an appreciation for a good pair of shoes."

Bill laughs and shakes my hand. Jack looks at us and I can sense a bit of confusion and possibly a bit of jealousy on his face. Sweet Jack has a jealous bone. I have to remember to investigate further into that. Note to self.

Bill goes on. "Nice to see you again, Sarah," then he turns to Jack. "I have those contracts that you need to sign. The clients want to break ground next week."

"Thanks, Bill. I will look them over and sign them this evening. Call Greg Willowbrook and tell him that we can set up a final meeting for the layouts so we can finalize the building structure."

"Will do." Bill turns to me and says, "Welcome aboard. Don't let Jack push you around too much. He can be a bit aggressive," he finishes with a laugh, then he turns to Jack, tips his hard hat and disappears out the door.

"Sounds like I should watch my back around you, Jack Calloway," I say, turning to him.

"That is the one thing you should not do." He walks up to me and clasps an arm around my waist, then he turns me to lead us deeper towards his office.

I think I'm going to enjoy working for him.

Chapter 17

Jack and I spend the next two hours going over blueprints of projects that have been put on hold since he has been so busy. It is quite impressive to see the types of clients that request Calloway Construction for their business. Not that I think he isn't worth every penny, but we are talking big-name clients. Jack has been working on a huge project and has been forced to put some projects on the shelf, for smaller 'ma and pop' clients, to focus on the bigger clients. He explains to me that it isn't the money that drives him, so his guilt for not completing these projects sits on his shoulders, but his clients are faithful to Calloway Construction and some go back from when his dad was around so they chose to wait it out, knowing it would be worth the wait.

He shows me a project that is in major need of a marketing plan. Jack has gotten around to designing the architectural plan for a kids' park for one of the smaller Chicago suburbs, but they need to be sold on the idea. His expertise is the design. How to sell it and market it to the city to get approved is where I come in.

It seems like the list goes on and on. This poor guy needed me eons ago! He shows me a restaurant project for an old building that I'm familiar with. The owners want to revamp it into a more modern restaurant and he has some ideas and prints, but again, he needs to sell the architecture in such a way that the client will see the vision. One after another, we go over each sitting project that needs some attention. With each one that he explains, I just light up more. This is going to be a piece of cake for me. He is offering me the opportunity to help create a vision for these clients who put their hard work and pay to create something for their community. By the time he is done showing me my options, I am gleaming with excitement.

"So what do you think? Is this something you can help me with?"

My smile is turned all the way up. "I think you came to the right place, Mr. Callaway. But I will forewarn you, I am not cheap," I state in a bit of seriousness.

Jack breaks the distance between us and tucks me into his arms. I wrap my arms around his neck, and he leans down to meet my gaze. Then he says, "I'm sure I will find a way to pay you as well as keep you very happy, Ms. Sullivan." He closes the remaining space between us and kisses me.

Chapter 18

As much as I want to stay behind closed doors with Jack all day and play *who can get naked faster*, I have a new passion and excitement on my hands. I couldn't even believe he was holding out on me with this! I was so excited to work on these projects I didn't even know where to begin. I had to convince Jack, which actually was a bit difficult, that we should put our necking on hold so I could get started on these plans right away.

I barely even talked to him while he drove me back to the house because I was so engrossed in looking at the plans and layouts. Idea after idea was overflowing in my head and I just couldn't get all my ideas down fast enough. It had been way too long since I was able to indulge in a good marketing plan.

We make it to the house, and I about jump out of the truck without even saying goodbye. Realizing quickly how rude I just was, I jump back in and slam a kiss on his lips.

"Thank you for this," I tell him. "I won't let you down."

"Should I be worried that I just unintentionally replaced myself in your head with work?" he asks jokingly.

"I'm a paid employee, Jack. It's important that I don't let my boss down. If you're lucky, maybe I will let you take me out again and you can tell me more about that bedroom that you built with your bare hands..."

"How do you know I built it with my bare hands?" he asks.

"Oh, because that's what I dream you're doing with those strong hands of yours when they aren't all over my body and inside places warm and inviting," I say, giving him the sweetest wink, and then I jump out of his truck.

I walk up the driveway, swaying my cute little ass because I know he is watching. Once I get to the door I turn around to see him staring at me with his mouth gaping open. I think I actually rendered Mr. Jack Calloway speechless! And with I'm sure a little aching in the private parts department. Well, good. Now we're even.

Chapter 19

Seven cups of coffee, three packages of pop tarts, and twelve hours later, I perfect the City Park project. It is crazy awesome. I am also exhausted and I believe semi-unconscious at my kitchen table. I hear distant voices, but I am pretty sure I am too tired to even bother to pull my eyes open.

"What is she doing?" I hear someone say.

"I'm not sure. I found her like this when I woke up this morning. I made a few attempts to wake her but she doesn't budge. Poor girl worked herself into a coma."

I identify voice #1 as Jack, and voice #2 as my mother. I am kind of hoping they will just go away or talk a bit quieter because I seriously need to get some sleep.

But knowing Jack, it doesn't take long before I feel his fingers wrap around my waist and pick me up into his arms. I crack open an eye and quickly shut it once the light strikes my vision.

"What are you doing?" I mumble into his shoulder. God, he smells good.

"I'm thinking about firing you, first of all. But most importantly I am carrying you to your bed so you can get some sleep in a place that doesn't consist of a chair and a table."

"I finished the City Park proposal."

"I bet you did."

"It's perfect."

"I'm sure it is."

"You're going to be very pleased with me."

"I wouldn't expect anything less from you."

"I'm probably going to ask for a raise."

"You don't even know what I'm paying you now…"

"Then you can just pay me with that sexy mouth of yours."

 I can feel Jack's chest vibrate while he laughs. Everything about Jack is turning out to be infectious. He makes it to my room and gently lays me on my bed and pulls up the covers.

"Sleep," he says while brushing a few strands of hair out of my face.

"Maybe just for a few minutes," I muffle out.

I am asleep in seconds.

Chapter 20

I wake up a bit groggy and confused about why I am dressed in my clothes and why my mouth is so dry. I don't think I hung out with Aunt Raines last night but one can never be too sure. I peel my tongue off the roof of my mouth and sit up. *What day is it?* Life starts returning to me, as my 'all-nighter' comes flooding back, along with my awesome accomplishment. I look on my nightstand and notice a note folded and sitting on the ledge. I open it:

Sarah,

I hope you were able to make up for the sleep you missed. I'm anxiously awaiting your City Project presentation. When you are up meet me at this address. I expect a very long and detailed presentation.

15412 Valley Drive - West Holland, Il 60502

-Jack

God, even his handwriting is attractive! I throw myself out of bed like a bat outta hell and head for the shower. This meeting sounds very serious. As in, I should probably shave all over—serious.

Everything in place, I set out to meet Jack. I choose my lucky gold stilettos because nothing can go wrong when you're in the trusting hands of a perfect shoe. I grab all my work and head out.

A bit nervous that I am headed the wrong direction, I end up on a long dirt road. Pretty certain I'm going to end up at the edge of a cliff soon, I finally start to see objects. As in a building of some sort. The closer I get the more I realize it's a house. Holy mother of hugeness, this is Jacks house?

There is no way that picture did it any justice. It is awesome! It sits on what has to be at least two acres of land. The structure is a ranch house with a porch wrapping around the whole house.

As I get close to the house, I can't even imagine someone building something so extraordinary. The house must be five of my parents' house put together. How does he live here all alone? *Does he live here alone?* I park quickly and get out of the car.

As I walk up to the house, I would be lying if I didn't feel for the first time a bit intimidated by what's been going on. All of this stuff with Jack has come out of nowhere. It is all happening so fast, but it's just so perfect. He has brought out so many positive emotions in me. Just thinking about him, it takes almost nothing to get my blood boiling with excitement. I step onto the porch and approach the door. I ring the bell in anticipation, almost debating turning around and running faster than hell back to the car like a Scaredy Cat. Too late.

Jack opens door right as I pivot to leave.

"Leaving so soon?" he asks, apparently figuring out my plan of action.

"Of course not. I figured you may have been in the shower, or changing, so I was going to find an open window and pull some Peeping Tom action." Or run...

"Uh huh," he says. "Come in. I've been waiting for you. Thought you were going to sleep through the week."

"Hey!" I bat him on the shoulder. "You're the one who forced me to go to sleep."

"Which you obviously needed."

We walk past the entryway, through the spacious living room into the open kitchen, and I stop. The scene in front of me leaves me speechless. Jack's kitchen is a huge open layout with white cabinets and dark granite countertops, all surrounding an island bar. The room connects to a sitting room that has a wall lined with bookshelves all stacked full. In the far end of the room, the fireplace is lit and inviting. And to the side, the whole wall is made of glass, which I'm assuming leads to the outside. But what takes my breath completely away are all the added features. Jack has laid out on the island bar a spread of food and wine, all surrounded by lit candles.

"What is all this?" I ask, astonished.

"Your raise," he says, pushing me forward.

"How do you know I deserve it?" I ask almost in a whisper.

"I'm going to take a leap of faith on you. And if it's bad, then I will make you repay me." He leans in and stops with this lips next to my ear. "And by repayment, I mean you finishing what you started earlier, by replaying for me that dream you had in complete, vivid detail."

Reminder to self: Breathe.

Jack leaves me to gape at his setup while he walks toward the counter and pours two glasses of wine. He returns and hands me a glass.

"Now, let's see what you are made of." He takes my hand and guides me down a hallway leading off the kitchen to what seems like a work area. In the back of the house he has another office which consists of a huge desk and a lit table, one would assume to illuminate blueprints. He takes my work and lays it all on the table and examines my notes and drawings. He is quiet for such a long time that I am starting to get a bit nervous that I got over my head and I wasn't as good as I thought I was—or that he thinks I am. I'm about to start lying and just say this was my rough draft and how I must have left the finished project at home, when he speaks—

"This is simply amazing."

Insert finally breathing and a towel for the bead of sweat that just formed on my forehead.

"You think so?" I ask casually. "'Cause if it's not I can always start—"

"You are amazing," he says. "This is perfect. In fact, this is more than perfect. It's like I had this vision and idea of how I wanted my architecture layout to be, and this was it. It's like you took exactly what I had formed in my head and put it on paper. The signs—" he pauses, "—everything."

Suddenly, Jack takes his phone from his back pocket, opens it and starts dialing a number. I'm a bit curious about who he needs to call at a time like this, but figure I will give him some privacy and turn to walk into the other room. He catches my arm and signals for me to stay.

"Hello, is William Frazier available, please? Yes, thank you. Yes, I'll hold."

He points to me and mouths, "Don't even think about moving."

"...Hello, Mayor Frazier...great, thanks for asking."

Holy basket case he is talking to the mayor right now?

"...I'm sorry for the odd hour to be calling. I wanted to let you know that I have finished the City Park layout and would like to set up a meeting with you and my associate to review the plans... Yes, and her work is impressive... I believe it will render you as speechless as it did me, Mayor... Great! We look forward to it. Have a nice evening." Jack hangs up and throws his phone on the desk. He looks at me and smiles. "Who *are* you?" he asks.

"Hey, that's my line!" I giggle a little. Feeling a bit self-conscious after all the attention, I try to turn to pay note to his office, but he grabs my arm and turns me around to face him again.

"What I want to know is where is this pathetic asshole of an ex of yours and how can I thank him for letting you go so I could get a chance?"

What? "What?"

"Sarah..." My name glides off his tongue like smooth silk. His stare heats up my face. I decide that it's a great time to try out this fancy wine and bring it to my lips. I take a huge gulp.

Knowing my plan for scapegoat by wine, he takes my glass and sets it down on the table. "I will not deny you your favorite hobby, but right now, I want to talk."

Oh boy. "Okay."

"What you just did here is incredible. This is going to make a lot of people very happy. If this is approved, and I cannot imagine why it wouldn't be, you just helped get a city park approved. Providing four surrounding towns with a communal play area for kids. These plans had to be perfect so the city council would approve it to be paid pro bono by the city. And there is no doubt you just made that happen."

Wow. "Wow."

"Wow is correct."

"Does this mean I get that raise?" I say, having to back up because Jack is slowly eliminating the space between our bodies.

"This means you get a raise..." he says in a low voice.

He gazes into my eyes and I just see the fire burning in his thoughts. He is so close now that I can feel his breath hit my face. It is intoxicating. "Beautiful..." he whispers, raising his hand to my face and using his thumb to caress my cheek.

"Is this the part where I get to see that hand-built bedroom of yours?"

Jack laughs. "Not so fast. I'm going to feed you first. Energy is a must in that bedroom." I think my mouth drops open, but I am too busy concentrating on my breathing to notice.

He leads me back into the kitchen and sits me down on one the bar stools. Then he refills my wine like a true hero would and begins laying out more assortments of cheeses, meats and fruits.

"I'm not sure what you like so I just threw some stuff together," he tells me. "I have steaks marinating, if you are OK with that."

I'm OK with anything you offer me. "Yeah," I say. "Sounds great."

Chapter 21

Growing some liquid courage, I open my mouth. "I'm sorry, but I have to ask. In front of me is this really great guy and I have to wonder, why are you even single? Or is it that I just haven't found evidence of the secret wife yet...or possibly girlfriend in another town?"

"Ha!" Jack laughs. "No. No secret wife or stashed away girlfriend. Nothing exciting really to tell. Had a pretty serious girlfriend in college. We had plans after college, but then Dad died, and I moved back home to take over his business permanently. She was from money, so her idea of 'plans' was not to live in the suburbs as a laborer's wife. When things were not going great, she was debating on moving on. Little did I know she was replacing me before that even happened. I'm not a fan of cheaters, or men who think they can just step in where they are not welcomed. Before we split, I could tell she was fishing for someone else. There would be times when we were out that she would flirt with other guys, just to see if she had a shot or, who knows, just to get a rise out of me. Eventually we went our separate ways. End of story. Haven't found the time to find a replacement since."

Holy wow. Poor jack!

"Oh, I'm sorry that happened to you, Jack. It sounds like you sacrificed a lot. With the company and your dreams, and everything."

"I chose this road. I had the choice to let it go or take it. I knew what I was risking and letting go when I chose this. It's better in the end anyway. I wouldn't want to be with someone who resented me later for the choices that I made. So, it was for the better. She loved money, and to be honest it means nothing to me. I'm sure in time that would have sent both of us packing in opposite directions."

We both sit in silence sipping our wine—well, Jack is sipping. I'm more like gulping. I feel so sad for Jack. Here I was always sulking on the 'poor me' card I was handed when he had lost everything himself. He gave up his dream and his future to continue his dad's legacy.

"How about this..." He breaks my thoughts. "How about I don't feel sorry for you if you do not feel sorry for me?"

"Deal," I say a bit embarrassed that he was able to read my thoughts.

Jack raises his glass, and I follow suit. "Cheers to the most remarkable person I have ever met. For accomplishing a goal off her list and completing a task, one I could not do without her."

We raise our glasses to meet and clink.

"Cheers to you for inspiring me."

"I do believe, Sarah, that is two that we can cross off," he says with a twinkle in his eye.

"You stand correct."

We smile and laugh and toast so much that I lose count. We talk about how the project that took me twelve hours to complete had been waiting to be started for almost a year. How the town's members have been sending letters to push the project for years but it kept getting denied because it 'just wasn't what the city had in mind'. I learn that Jack is actually three years older than me, at thirty-four. We finish off the bottle of wine and Jack opens another. We sit and talk while he grills the steaks and we eat on his back patio, so I can admire the view. It's crazy how, when you take away a neighborhood of crammed houses and pollution, the sky is so beautiful at night. After helping with the dishes, Jack puts some music on, and the sultry sounds fill the room.

He grabs me by the waist and swings me into his body to dance with him. I follow suit by wrapping one arm around his waist and one arm over his shoulder. He leads me into a slow dance, while the music plays through the speakers.

"Have I thanked you yet for hitting my car?" He slows his movements and spins me. "There is something about you that I can't stop thinking about. Ever since I spotted you in my rearview mirror that day. I haven't thought of anything since. Your smile, your laugh, your addiction to vermouth, which I'm still trying to understand—"

"Hey," I say defensively. "The vermouth is Aunt Raines' addiction. I'm just trying to keep up. Aren't we supposed to take a page out from our elders?"

He spins me again and pulls me closer into his body.

"I just can't fathom how anyone would let you go. If you were mine, I would cherish you, spoil you rotten and never let you out of my sight…"

At the last word to leave his mouth I am already slamming my mouth on his. I can't get to him fast enough. All the words he is speaking are floating in my head and almost cutting off the air supply to my brain. I just want to hold on, almost afraid that if I let go he will disappear. His mouth is too inviting. I pull back and find his eyes. "You're real, right?" I have to ask. This is not my reality. Someone like this doesn't just come into my life and turn everything upside-down, but in a good way. I feel it to the core of my heart that he is something I should have found a long time ago. He hasn't been in my life for that long, but I feel it. I feel the beginning stages of something powerful.

"I'm as real as you are, baby," he whispers then dips forward where I want him most, his lips touching mine.

And then we explode. All four hands don't even know what to do with themselves. We are both clawing at each other to get closer. I can feel my lips bruising from the intense pressure of our kiss. The need in both of us is unbearable.

Without thought, Jack picks me up and throws me over his shoulder. Breathing heavily, he walks down the hallway and then through a double-framed doorway. He pushes through the doors and leads me into the room.

The bedroom.

I can tell by the gigantic four-poster framed king-sized bed, dark wood covered with a light grey duvet. The bed is unreal. From what I can see without losing focus on Jack, it is a bed made for never leaving. And I'm hoping my theory stands correct.

Jack sets me down on the plush mattress and pulls my legs towards the edge of the bed. He stops me once the back of my legs hang over the bed. I can tell he is struggling to keep control. His hands are pressed into my thighs. He leans forward and begins to kiss me again but at a much slower pace than before.

He unhurriedly moves his hands upward and inside my shirt, where he latches onto the hem of the shirt and pushes upward while caressing my skin with every move. Knowing where this is going, I lift my arms. He carefully slides my shirt up and over my head.

My shirt drops to the floor next to my feet. He continues his inspection of my body by moving his hands up my stomach and grazing his thumbs across my covered nipples. That move earns a moan from both our mouths.

With ease, Jack then drops to his knees. He presses his thumbs into the sides of my hips and brushes soft kisses along my stomach, traveling downward towards my navel, and ending just above my jeans' line.

The way he touches me is so tender, my body is reacting in waves of pleasure. I lift my hands and glide my fingers through his hair. The simple gesture delivers another moan from Jack.

With every kiss that he brushes along my skin, he looks up to lock eyes with me. I can literally see the passion radiating off him. Gazing into Jack's eyes is like looking into a portal. Seeing a man who is warm and inviting. One that can make me content for a lifetime. I can't wrap my thoughts around how I went from being so stricken to so lucky.

He breaks my thoughts by softly biting my thigh through my jeans.

Oh holy burning hunk of foreplay, I am so turned on. I want him to take his time and touch me all over my body, but then again, I want to help him rip my pants off and just head straight for home base.

He must be reading my thoughts because I feel the buttons being snapped open as my jeans, along with my panties, go south. He tosses more clothes into the growing pile on the floor.

Jack stands up in an animal prowl sort of way and starts to move forward. I let him guide me back so my legs still hang over the bed but my back is now lying flat on the plush mattress. He stops to take in my naked lower body with his eyes. He groans.

"You are so fucking beautiful," Jack says in a raspy growl. Then he places his hands on my hips and gently pulls me forward so my girly parts are sitting right at the edge. He leans over me and presses his lips to mine. I can feel the urge in his kiss. He breaks away and slowly drops to his knees again. "You smell so good. I want to smell all of you." *Oh god, he is going to—.* Just as I try to finish my thought, Jack lowers his head and places his mouth in-between my legs. I can feel the heat of his breath hitting my inner thighs, tiny little breaths away from my lips. He takes his hands from my waist and moves down to press them into my thighs. Every kiss he places on my inner thigh sends a jolting tingle to my center. I think this guy is going to make me explode before he actually even touches me.

And then he does.

Jack finally takes his tongue and swipes it along my lips. "Ahhhhhh..." I groan as I throw my head back in complete pleasure. One lick after another he works his way to the center of my bud. Every stroke sends me more over the edge, toward explosion. I stab my fingers into his hair and grip for dear life. He continues to lick my center as he slowly enters me with one finger. I moan loudly at the feel of him inside and almost break at the feeling. He pulls his finger out and inserts it again. This time I feel two. *Holy god all mighty.*

"God, you are so wet, Sarah." *And about to explode if he keeps this up.* Hearing my name flow off his tongue while he drives my body wild is too much.

"Oh Jack…" I moan and I feel my orgasm on the brink exploding. I sense he feels it too, because he abruptly pulls out. He stands, and in one quick movement, rips his shirt over his head. He unbuttons his jeans and with a swift tug, pulls them down along with his boxers. How someone can get undressed so fast is pure amazement and also so fucking hot. While he's standing naked in front of me, I am finally able to get a good look at his fully naked body. Holy god, he is all muscle, and smooth, and tan, and… Wow…

I mean, WOW!

I am so turned on by him right now that my mouth literally starts to water. If he doesn't make a move soon, I may attack him. He sees the hunger in my eyes, and picks my body up and pulls me to the center of the bed. He covers my body with his and slams his mouth onto mine. I taste myself on his lips and it drives me wild. I feel his hard length on my stomach and I cannot wait to have him inside me. He seems to read my mind again, and I feel his knee nudging my legs open. He lifts his hips and I can feel his hard length at my core. With a lustful shove he enters me whole, which sends my head flying back. We moan in unison as he begins to move inside me.

"God you feel so good, Sarah..." he groans as he kisses my neck and moves back up to my lips. I can feel his hands roaming up my stomach. He cups one of my breasts and bends his head down to wrap his mouth around my nipple.

"Oh god Jack, yes..." I am done for. Every thrust that Jack offers sends me further into oblivion. I can feel my orgasm start to surface. Jack lets go of my nipple to move on to the other one. His repeat performance gets another moan from me. This is it. Thrust for thrust, the pressure swells into my center and I scream out his name, while ecstasy blows up around me.

"Yeah baby, I can feel you clenching. Come for me." The way Jack is talking to me is too much. I feel him speed up his rhythm and his thrust gets deeper and more aggressive. Before I know it I am well on my way to another orgasm. Jack can sense this too. He takes his hand and lowers it to my bud and begins to rub it while pounding into me. I am done. Two more thrusts and I again start screaming his name. Shortly after, I feel Jack throw his head back and groan loudly, letting go.

Jack's body gives in and falls onto mine. The feeling of pure pleasure is exhausting. I can feel his rapid heartbeat thumping out of his chest. Mine is doing the same. What was that? I just had a back-to-back orgasm? Who is this guy?

We are both trying to steady our breathing. His weight is heavy but I love the feel of his hard body pressed against mine. I take whatever energy I have left and wrap my legs around his hips to keep the contact. I want to stay molded to him forever.

As our breathing evens out, Jack shifts and flips onto his back, taking me with him. Lying on top, I lift my head to catch his eyes taking me in, his expression of complete fulfillment.

"Who are you?" I whisper slowly. I watch the corners of his mouth rise into a pure, satisfied grin.

"Someone who's about to get real poor with all the raises I plan on giving out."

I break out into a loud laugh. Jack squeezes me again and flips. I'm now below his body, and he looks at me with hunger, already building desire to fulfill more of his cravings.

"I think I'm going to have to retract my subcontractor contract, and hire you on full time."

"Then you're definitely going to go broke." I giggle.

"It will be worth every penny."

We both laugh. Then he dips his head down again to press a soft kiss to my lips.

Chapter 22

Five hours later and four more repeats of me seeing stars, I wake up to the sun forcing its way into my eyelids. I slowly open my eyes. A bit confused by my surroundings, I lift my head to see a warm body tangled up next to me.

Jack.

In Jack's bedroom.

Glorious.

He looks so peaceful in his sleep. Take away the lines of wear and tear in his face that I notice during the days he pushes himself with work, and he looks a lot younger than he is. I take a finger and brush away a piece of hair that is loose on his head and hanging over his eyebrow.

He stirs in his sleep and his arm quickly wraps around my neck, pulling me back down to the shared pillow he has his head resting on.

His eyes slowly open and a smile broadens across his face. He is simply amazing.

"Good morning," he says with a deep half-awake voice.

"Good morning."

He raises his hand and guides my head closer to meet his and then locks his beautiful lips to mine. It is nothing erotic or crazy, but it is simple. And beautiful. It feels like we have been waking up like this for a lifetime, and not just for the first time.

"So I have an idea," he says, breaking into my thoughts.

"Oh yeah?"

"I have some client meetings on site today. I want you to work in my office. You can have access to all the materials that you would need to work on the plans. It will beat using your kitchen table as a work bench slash nesting place."

"I thought you just said that you have meetings. Won't you need your office to conduct those?"

"No. I can use the main room upfront. I want you there all day with me. I want to make sure I can check up on you anytime I want throughout my day... And let me follow that up with, if you say no, then I will be forced to cancel all my meetings and find a reason to observe my men on their 'addition project' today."

I take a moment to look at him and debate my options. Both options seem to entail Jack tending to my whereabouts. Either option doesn't sound like I will be allowed very much concentration.

"Well, boss, with all the money I am costing you, I would hate to see you lose business on my behalf."

He laughs into my hair and begins to press kisses to my neck. "Good." Then he jumps off me and out of bed. He grabs the covers and throws them to the bottom of the bed. Feeling a bit self-conscious, I go to grab for them. "Oh no you don't," he says.

He grabs my arm, gently but assertively, and lifts me up off the bed.

"What are you doing?" I ask in a bit of a panic.

"Getting you ready for work. You have a busy day ahead of you."

He proceeds to pick me up and carry me to the bathroom. He goes to the shower and turns on the water. Checking to make sure it's a decent temperature, he sets me down. I would tell you that he threw off his clothes, or mine, but we weren't wearing any...

Jack presses his hands around my hips and guides me into the shower with him. We turn together to face the water and he presses his lips to mine. Who would have thought that morning showers could be so enthralling? I'm seeing stars.

Again.

As in *twice.*

Chapter 23

Jack drives me back to my parents' house, since I need to pick up the projects he gave me, and probably put a fresh pair of clothes on. I am currently residing in my jeans and an oversized, crisp shirt complimentary of Jack's closet. If I said I wasn't going to take this shirt off and turn it into my new pillowcase, I would be lying. Going to bed and waking up with the scent of Jack on my face sounds heavenly to me.

Jack holds my hand the whole way. His phone keeps ringing with clients calling, suppliers confirming orders, and workers signing in and out. He refuses to let my hand go to maneuver his phone, so he uses the speaker device to talk. It is probably a good thing that he's so occupied with driving and talking, because I'm pretty sure if anyone takes a good look at me they would see a girl as giddy and happy as a kid in a candy store...and oh, who also just won the candy lottery.

We pull up to the house and he signals that he will be a minute, which is my cue to exit. I enter the house, hoping my mom isn't on duty and I can make a clean break to my room without being questioned by the parent police.

No. Such. Luck.

"Hi honey, I'm glad to see you home. How was your night?"

Please someone explain to my conscious that I am thirty-one years old and don't need to feel like I'm about to get grounded for not coming home last night. I mean, if I'm going to look like a hussie to my parents, then, well, so be it!

"Um… Great, Mom. We had a lot of work that we had to go over. A lot of projects." Lie. "I'm just going to change and grab my work stuff. Jack needs me to work at his site today. More materials to help me work." Why did I not sound convincing?

"OK, dear. That Jack fellow sure knows what he is doing," my mom responds to my departing back.

She has no idea.

Chapter 24

Speeding up to the good part, which doesn't take too long, I find myself in Jack's office playing with the restaurant revamp project. It takes about twenty-seven minutes alone in his office before the door opens then shuts with a clicking sound. I turn to see Jack walking my direction with clear intention in his eyes.

"I thought you were in a meeting?" I barely manage to ask the whole question before he grabs my waist and crushes my body into his.

"I am. They are looking over some numbers. I told them to take their time. I had to attend to a private matter."

He dips his head and presses his mouth to my neck. I can feel his warm breath on my skin, and I instantly melt into his embrace. This guy is going to be the death of me. Grazing his tongue along my neck, making his way to my mouth, he speaks. "How is the assignment coming along my little employee?"

He's going to kill me. "It's going—" *Oh mother of suction*, he just started nibbling on my ear.

"It's going what, Sarah?"

My brain is spitting out words, but I'm not sure my mouth is relaying them. I can tell at this point that my mouth is hanging open. I also conclude that the only thing coming out of my mouth are tiny moans.

"If you keep making those sweet noises, I'm going to have to clear my schedule for the rest of the day."

I want to say *don't bother*, since I'm pretty sure he has kissed and nibbled me unconscious. Not sure what use I would be at this point.

A knock on the door sends my eyes fluttering open. Jack's eyes are on me when I resume focus, and I can see the fire in his gaze.

"Jack?"

On the other side of the door is Bill. "Breaking Ridge is done reviewing the numbers. They are ready to move forward."

Jack sighs. "I'll be right out."

We both stand there looking at each other while listening to Bill's steps as they disappear into the distance.

"You are lucky," he tells me. "The things I had planned for you were not very appropriate in an office, especially with clients outside the door."

I need to get a hold of my jaw because it just seems to drop down on its own lately.

Jack laughs and brings his hand up to graze my cheek. "I'll let you get back to work. Although you do inspire me to have the quickest meetings I've ever had so I can be done with this day and finish this other...private matter."

Nope, I'm not talking yet. Still staring and gaping.

Jack just smiles, brushes a kiss to my lips, and turns to leave. I hear the door open and shut, but cannot say that I am aware of anyone leaving. I am too busy staring. And gaping. Still.

Chapter 25

I actually didn't see much of Jack the rest of the day. His meetings turned into a bigger commotion than I assume he planned on. Clients were in and out with prospective work proposals and negotiations all day.

I can't say I didn't miss the feel of Jack's hands all over my body, but the absence did allow me to focus and get a solid start on the restaurant project. The plans were unreal. I couldn't grasp why Jack had been stalling on all these projects. Each one I picked up was already pretty complete, with exception to the marketing plan and layout of advertising and the boost to get it to sell.

The restaurant plan was a no-brainer. I looked at the design Jack had put together. The restructure of the restaurant would offer the owner more seating and push back the kitchen, which would also grow in space. The floor structure allowed easier access for staff to rotate and an open view of the street activity. The location was set in a popular place in the city but the outside of the building killed the business. The old building lacked in ventilation and the old beams and structure restricted space for tables and expanded seating. The project was completed up till the outside signage structure and the design of the marketing plan. Everything Jack had already created was to the tee, the same input I would have done. It was incredible. The only thing the plans were missing was the outside sex appeal to fellow foodies.

The clock dings five o`clock when I finally lift my nose out of my drawings. I look back at what I completed and am very impressed. The accomplishment feels so good. I missed this stuff. I missed the drive and the satisfaction of being good at something. I missed watching my work turn into real life building signs, or product logos. Walking into a clothing store and seeing the display put together, knowing that was once just a drawing on a piece of paper originating from my mind.

At that moment, Jack enters his office. He looks exhausted. He walks my way and takes a seat, or more like flops into the chair next to me.

"You look exhausted," I say, focusing on his tired expression.

"Have dinner with me."

"What?"

"I said have dinner with me".

"Are you asking me or telling me?" I ask in attempt to be witty and cute.

Jack laughs. "Well I'm asking of course. I do have manners. I got a call from Mayor Frazier today and he wants to sit down over dinner and look over the final plans. I want you to be there. This wouldn't have been completed if it wasn't for you."

Holy... I get to meet the mayor!

"Well I'm not sure," I tell him. "I feel like it's not really my place. Don't you think you should just go? I mean, I don't want to intrude."

"Sarah—" He says my name while grabbing my hands. He pulls me over to him and sits me down to straddle his lap. "You will not be intruding. You will save me from a boring dinner, as well as show off your talent. I won't take no for an answer."

A jolt of excitement flows through me. I smile and lean in to brush a kiss against Jack's lips. I lift my head. "Fine, you have yourself a dinner date."

Jack doesn't miss a beat. He grabs the back of my neck to guide my head down for another kiss.

We finally break apart, both a bit winded, and Jack speaks. "You are going to be the death of me."

"You're telling me..."

Chapter 26

Hand in hand, Jack leads me through the glass doors of the swanky steakhouse. A bit nervous to be at a sit-down dinner with the mayor, I decide to make an exception and dig through my burn-at-first-chance pile of ex-Hamilton work attire for something to wear. I decide on an exquisite silk blouse and grey pencil skirt, complementing it with my favorite charcoal blazer. Since an outfit is not complete without its shoe pairings, I choose my best black Jimmy Choos. Jack seems to have the same idea and is dressed in a charcoal button-up shirt and a black blazer. He wears jeans still, but the way they snuggle his backside, I'm not sure it matters what he wears. No one will be looking at anything else.

Before reaching the hostess stand, Jack leans down and brushes a kiss on my cheek. "You look exquisite."

I thought so myself!

"Thank you, so do you. Those jeans—"

The hostess takes that instant to rudely interrupt our moment. Eyeing Jack like a hungry wild panther, she takes our names. "Oh yes, Mr. Calloway. The mayor is waiting for you in the private dining room. Please let me take you back." She finishes and gives him the 'I'm single and very available' look and turns to guide us back through the restaurant. Seriously?! What is wrong with people? I don't want to have to admit that I am kind of jealous right now, because that would be silly. I mean she is just a hostess, and if I noted, Jack doesn't seem fazed by her. But still. Note to self: Put a 'taken' sign on Jack's forehead.

Not that he is taken. I mean. Is he taken?

Dinner turned out to be fantastic! Who would have thought the mayor was so laid back and comical? We sat while listening to his stories most likely in an attempt to sell us on some of his future campaigns. The whole time, Jack held my hand, periodically brushing his thumb over the inside of my wrist. I'm glad I didn't overdue it on the blush tonight because I'm sure my cheeks were naturally flushed the whole time. Dessert came, and of course the female waitress practically sat her boobs in Jack's face, while setting his plate in front of him. Jack didn't seem to take awareness.

"...Sarah, I can't express enough, these ideas are magnificent. If I was the only member on the counsel I would approve this immediately," the mayor praises while looking over the portfolio I put together.

"Thank you," I say. "I hope it gets approved. It would be a great accomplishment to offer a community such a beautiful park."

"I must agree with you, Ms. Sullivan. I know Jack's work and that's why I chose him for the project. May I ask where you mysteriously came from? What's your background?"

I know before the end of that sentence is pulled from his mouth where it is going. I tense up instantly. Jack catches it and under the table he squeezes my hand.

"I spent a few years working as a Marketing Director for Hamilton Corp in downtown Chicago. After seven years, I felt my time there was up and I needed to expand my wings and see what else was out there for me. That's when I met Jack, and he offered me this opportunity."

"Wow, Hamilton Corp. That's impressive. I just had lunch with Hamilton's son yesterday. That Steve Hamilton. He has an impressive background as well. Are you familiar with him?"

Insert nausea now.

Was I familiar...

"Yes, I've worked on a few projects with Steve." I can't really say any more without negative feelings spreading across my face. I start to chew on the inside of my cheek to hold back any emotion.

I'm sure Jack notices too.

Dinner wraps up shortly after that and we are exiting the restaurant. "Thank you again, Sarah. I hope you will stick around longer and continue to make your mark on our town and city projects."

"Thank you mayor, that's very kind of you," I say in return with a bit of blush rising in my face.

"You keep that Calloway fellow in check now. He's a good boy. His father and I go way back. Fine talent that family produces."

At this I glance at Jack who is now looking embarrassed. "I will do my best."

We say our good-byes and part ways.

Jack helps me into the truck. Instead of shutting the door, he grabs my legs and pivots my body so my feet are now dangling outside.

"Are you OK?" he asks with a hint of concern in his tone.

"I'm fine, thank you."

"I mean are you OK from what he brought up in there?"

"Sure, it's no big deal. His company is well known around here. I can't avoid hearing of it, or of him."

Jack's smile is a mile wide. "You were wonderful in there. The more time I spend with you, the more I see just how amazing you are. I feel the need to take you home and lock you away so I don't have to share you with anyone."

I think I just mentally fainted.

"I didn't pin you for a kidnapper, Jack."

"Oh, you'd be surprised at the things I would do, if it meant keeping you in arm's length."

Here we go again with the fainting. If I could have left my body at this moment, it would be smack on the floor unconscious.

"I know you have a busy day of work tomorrow and a very demanding boss. How about if I promise to put in a good word, you come back to my place and we can celebrate your victory?"

We can celebrate right here if you undress me fast enough.

"That would be great," I simply say.

Chapter 27

I make it through the threshold of Jack's house. I hear the door shut, and quick steps behind me. I feel his hand wrap around my waist and spin me into his chest. He slams his mouth so fast onto mine that my breath escapes me. The heat from both our bodies is colliding and I can tell just how badly Jack wants to celebrate. I'm not sure if it is coming from him or myself, but I hear tearing and ripping as we both frantically scratch at either's clothes in an effort to get them off. I latch onto Jack's shirt and pull it up, revealing his tanned rock-hard abs. I fiddle with the buttons but can't stop shaking long enough to get one open. Jack on the other hand is winning the race. He grabs at my shirt and rips the front open, busting three buttons right off, and then lifts my arms to throw it over my head. I am so turned on at this moment; I can climax simply by looking at the face and body in front of me.

"You drive me completely mad," he says, his voice hoarse with hunger. You wouldn't even know he just ate a full four-course meal.

I give up on his shirt and start for his jeans buttons. Those seem a bit easier since I just pull and tear them open. This is insane. We are like two crazed animals fighting to get to the naked touch faster.

He grabs my mouth and sends it crashing again into his. When I am secure around his mouth he uses his hands to lift up my butt and wrap my legs around his waist. Without breaking our kiss, he walks forward, down the hall and to the bedroom.

He stops at the end of the bed and not so gently tosses me onto it. I land on my back with my hair spilling around my head. I look up to meet Jack's hungry stare.

He looks so predaceous at this point, there is no way of getting out of this alive. As in, without being tamed to death by hot Jack sex.

He climbs onto the bed and presses his body on top of mine. He makes contact with me and dips his head to press his lips aggressively to mine.

After ravishing my mouth, Jack lifts his head and again looks at me. "It is simply impossible to get enough of you."

Then he lowers his mouth to my neck, and makes a trail of burning kisses down my collarbone and to my breasts. My back arches at the feel of his hot breath on my skin. At this rate we are not even going to have to do the deed for me to explode.

Like a treasure map, he follows a trail of want down my stomach to my navel. Taking a little bite on my lower stomach, he leans up to unfasten my skirt. I lift up my hips to help him as he eases off my skirt, taking my panties with it.

He stops his feast of my skin for a moment and stares at my body. I see his green eyes disappear and black orbs forming in a wild hunger. "Now this is the dessert I have been waiting for," he mutters, then dips his mouth onto my goods.

Holy Hottie McTongue God.

My hips buckle instantly. His mouth on me there is just simply the most exotic thing I have ever felt. His tongue thrashing is driving me to the brink of complete insanity. Just when I think I am going to black out from pure pleasure, he again abruptly pulls away.

I open my eyes. Jack moves upward and is now leaning above me. At some point he has taken off his pants and is now completely naked. He adjusts his body so he is fully on top of me. Using his knee, he spreads open my legs. He doesn't meet any resistance since I gladly open up nice and wide.

With a hint of desire in his smile, he presses down and enters.

The fullness of him is so intense, we both growl instantly. And I mean *growl*. The feeling of him inside me is unimaginable. The fullness and his movements are making me insane with need. I wrap my legs around him to close any space that is left between us and follow with every thrust. Jack's hands skim up the side of my body to land on my breast. He cups my breast in his hand and squeezes. The sensation rips through me like a thunderstorm. I pick up both arms and thread my fingers into his hair. He moans in my mouth and picks up speed with his movements. I can tell we are both on the brink of exploding. Our hearts are beating so hard against each other's chests.

Right before the last thrust, I buckle my hips and scream Jack's name into his mouth. I throw my head back and see stars, while riding out my climax. Jack rumbles my name while he presses into me once more then goes down his own pleasurable path of ecstasy.

Jack, now on his back, is breathing heavily. I, on the other hand, am not sure if I am even alive. I think I am breathing but this all has to be a dream. There is no way something that incredible just happened to me, awake. I pinch myself. "Ouch," I say in a struggled whisper.

"You OK over there?" he asks, his voice sounding just as strained as mine.

"Oh yeah, just great. I needed to pinch myself to make sure that just happened and I wasn't dreaming."

Jack chuckles and turns on his side. He places his arm on my stomach and adjusts his hand to cup my boob.

Oh yeah. He's real. I feel that.

"You know, I should have wrote 'seeing stars' on my list of things I wanted to accomplish. I would have been able to scratch one more goal off my list."

Jack laughs again. Then he jumps up and throws his body over mine. He leans in and presses a tender kiss to my lips. He works his magic and I open my mouth so our tongues connect. Not wasting a second, he starts to get my body aching all over again. I wrap my limp arms around his neck and hold on.

Not breaking the kiss, he takes one of my hands and brings it down so it is resting on my stomach. Using his hand as a guide, he takes my fingers and begins rubbing circles on my lower abdomen. I start to ache all over at this gesture. He slowly moves lower into my privates and guides my fingers to my golden spot. I cannot say that I have ever been this intimate with someone in my life. I would have thought this action would have embarrassed me but it's turning me on even more. He takes my finger and makes a circling motion on my hot spot and I can't help but press my hips into both our hands. I hear myself moan just before he guides my finger inside.

Taking his time, he inserts one of my fingers as well as his own. He slowly pulls out, and then repeats this welcoming assault on my body. I am again at my peak of desire, when he pulls out completely.

I look down at his face, his expression pleased.

"What are you doing?" I ask in frustration.

"Marking off another notch on your list," he responds eagerly.

"And which one is that?"

"Finding yourself," he says in a rugged whisper, and plunges our fingers back home.

I come instantly.

Chapter 28

I wake up just as fast as I fell asleep. Jack did a serious number on me last night. I am pretty sure I passed out while pulling off of him. Two full nights of sexual exercise has been tiring. I know that he isn't in the bed with me because I don't feel the heat from his body radiating off me. I am lying on my stomach, spread out, and begin to smile in his pillow. I can smell his scent. Like fresh rain and men's cologne, and just sexy.

I start to think about all the great things that have happened in the last couple of weeks. Who would have thought that so fast, my life would have turned around? All because of Jack. He was giving me my life back bit by bit. I could also not deny the fuzzy feeling I got in my stomach whenever I thought of him. And his strong hands. His beautiful words when he spoke to me. The way he looked at me with deep want and longing. I knew there was one thing that was slowly being crossed off my list. And whether he felt it or not, I was definitely getting to remember what it felt like to fall in love again.

Chapter 29

Eager to sleep the day away, but more curious about where Jack is, I set out to find him. I pick up one of his shirts he has left on the bed, assuming for me, and head towards the kitchen. I smell the coffee before I make it into the kitchen and groan. My second love.

I walk into the kitchen, barefoot and swimming in Jack's shirt. Jack isn't in the kitchen but I can hear his distant voice coming from the back office. I go to the cabinets and open a couple before I spot his stash of mugs.

While pouring a hefty cup, I spot the powdered creamer and sugar. Caffeine concoction complete, I venture towards Jacks office.

I step through the door to see Jack's back facing me, while he's leaning over his workbench. Hearing my entrance, he turns around and looks my way. The smile that grows on his face is enough to make my knees shake. He holds his finger up to signal me to wait, while he finishes up his phone call.

"No. I want the report by this afternoon. I don't care that it's Friday. I am out of town this weekend and I won't have access to any fax. I need them signed before I leave. Thank you. Keep me posted. Goodbye."

Where is Jack going this weekend? I think with a resigned sadness because he will be away for so long. He didn't mention that he was planning a trip.

"Good morning," he says putting his phone on his workbench and making his way towards me.

"Good morning. I'm sorry I slept so late, you should have woken me."

"If I would have woken you, I would have just tired you out again. And you looked like you needed your rest."

My face goes flush instantly and I can feel the warmth in my cheeks. Jack just laughs and scoops me in for a hug. I love being in his arms. I wrap my arms around him and nestle my face into his chest.

"So you're headed out of town this weekend?" I say it before I think. I shouldn't have made it known that I was listening to his call. I feel so stupid. "I'm sorry, it's none of my business—"

He cuts me off. " I am not going anywhere." He pulls away so he can look me in the eyes. "*We* have plans. I wanted to clear up some loose ends with clients so I am not bothered all weekend."

God I think I love you.

"Oh." I stand corrected.

"I'm also giving you the day off. I have one more phone call to make then I'm going to drop you off at your house. I want you to pack some things so you are comfortable and we are going to have an extended sleepover at my place. If that's OK with you?"

Is the sky blue??

"I think I can manage this," I say while my inner self dances in circles.

"Good. Now get ready to go. And put some pants on. 'Cause I'm about two seconds away from taking my shirt back and having my way with you for breakfast."

He pretends to dart at me and I flinch out of the way. He starts to laugh and then his phone rings.

I let him take his call and head back to his room to collect my things.

Chapter 30

This is what it feels like to be a teenager again! Before dropping me off, Jack and I immaturely make out in his truck in his driveway. We cannot seem to go even a few moments without throwing ourselves at one another. Knowing that the best is yet to come, we control our hormones long enough to get me home. After Jack drops me off I walk inside hoping to avoid my parents. It's not easy being a thirty-one-year-old walking in the house like it's a walk of shame. I tiptoe to the stairs, and then I hear it.

"Honey? Is that you?"

Fail.

"Yes, Mom?"

"Two very large packages came for you early this morning. You might want to take a peek at it."

Now she's got my attention. I walk into the kitchen and on the table sits the biggest bouquet of red roses I have ever seen. There has to be close to...seven dozen. My mouth drops open.

Seven Dozen...

The amount of time we were together. And red. His favorite color. I start to feel sick.

"Honey, you look so pale. Are you feeling OK?" my mother asks.

"Uh. I'm fine. When did these come?" I ask. How did he know where I was? I mean it's not like I was in hiding, but still.

"They came this morning. There is a card on it. I'm sure it will explain who they are from." Like my mom nor myself doesn't already know where they came from.

My mom met Steve on numerous occasions. He would invite my parents to the city for dinners and cocktail events. He would wine and dine them, but never once did he make it when my parents invited him to their home for a nice family sit-down. That just wasn't Steve. His family sit-down version was a twelve-course dinner with a butler and fancy things. My parents never showed that it bothered them but it was obvious they were hurt. "The man who is dating our daughter can't come to a blue collar household and sit down for a roast?" That's what my dad would always say. I couldn't even blame him. He was right.

I jump back to reality and reach for the card. I feel sick even touching it. My nerves and anxiety do a 100% spike in the radar. My hands are shaking as I open the card. I don't even know what it is going to say. I am not sure what I want it to say.

I unfold the card and read:

Sarbear,

I miss you. I miss us.

Steve.

I can't do much but stare at it. So much is going through my head that I can't even grasp onto one thought to process. Why now? It's been months!? Why is he choosing to reach out now? He misses me? I am going to be sick. At what point did he decide that he missed me? When he realized he cheated on me!? When he got sick of Stacey?! Did he have some sick sixth sense that knew I was happy so he decided to ruin it for me!? I'm not sure when my mom decided to leave me to my thoughts but when I look around at the kitchen, it is empty and drowning in flowers.

My mom walks back into the kitchen from the back and looks at me in a worried state. "Honey, your second package is outside on the back porch. He insisted on waiting for you."

What the hell?

"Who is it?" I ask even though I know. It's not just a who. It's a *him*.

How did he find me?

I stand shell-shocked. What the mother effen hell is he doing at my parents' house?! He's never stepped foot in the suburbs and now he is on my back porch?!

I walk to the back of the kitchen and exit out the back door. I look at the beautiful patio and addition that Jack and his crew have built and see Steve on it. My anger thickens.

"What are you doing here?" is all I can manage to spit out.

He turns abruptly, not expecting my harsh tone. "You were not returning any of my calls. I had to see you."

Calls? Oh yeah! My phone! I haven't had my phone since weeks ago... Since Jack.

"I got rid of my phone," I retort.

"Can we talk? I miss you. I'm sorry but I need you to hear me out," he says with a bit of begging in his voice.

"I am not sure I have anything to say to you, Steve. You shouldn't have come here," I say, expressing more anger and a little more struggle to my voice.

"I wouldn't have come if you would have just called me back."

"How *dare* you just show up at my parents' house thinking that you can just ask things of me! You have no right to me anymore, Steve," I snap back, though I'm inwardly hoping I do not break down and cry.

"I know. Sar, I need you to understand. I love you. Please. Just listen." I do not know what to do in this situation. My emotions are on high alert right now and I am not sure how much fight I have in me. I sit down on the lawn chair and wait for him to speak.

He sits down at the end of the chair and faces me. I feel a sudden urge of uncomfortableness and am regretting even addressing him.

"I want you to know that I broke things off with Stacey. I mean... I didn't break anything off. There was nothing to break off. It was a one-time thing."

I stare are him in complete disbelief. He catches my vibes, and retracts.

"OK, I'm sorry it was more than once, but it didn't mean anything. She was always all over me, and I'm sorry I was weak. I just gave in. I hate myself for what I've done to you. To us. I miss you, Sarbear. You have to believe me. I am miserable without you."

Just having to listen to him call me by the nickname he gave me is painful. Listening to the details start to make me shake. I begin to feel sick all over again. Just when I finally bury all these bad truths about what they did to me, here he is creating fresh wounds.

"Why, Steve? Why? I gave you everything," I say in a strangled voice. I am about to let myself break down and cry. He attempts to move closer to me, and I put my hand up to stop him. "Don't."

"Sar. Please. I love you. I cannot explain how sorry I am. Please come back to me. We can work this out. I can talk to my father and work out something with your job. Stacey is done. Please."

He then puts his hand on my chin to lift my face so I am able to make eye contact with him. I stare into his eyes and try to find guilt or remorse in there somewhere. I see the face of a man I thought I loved for seven years until he tore me apart. I feel a tear run down my face. He brushes the tear away with his thumb and bends forward, swiftly placing a kiss to my lips.

I feel the touch of his lips and his mouth on mine but what is missing is that spark. The feeling that in my heart I know it fits. The way I feel when Jack's lips are touching mine. It takes mere seconds to know there is nothing there for me anymore.

"Stop!" I exclaim, and push his mouth away from my face.

"Why? I thought you wanted this. Wanted us?" he asks in an almost annoyed tone. "You wouldn't leave my side when we were together. I know you love me. Don't act like this isn't what you want, Sarah. We can work this out. Move past this. We are adults."

He is clearly in denial and I am about to go apeshit. His selling speech to get me back has turned into making note of my weaknesses while we were together. How could I have not seen what an ass he was before?

I stand up and wipe my mouth with my sleeve. "Get off my porch, Steve. And do not come back here."

"Sarah, come on. Talk to me. I'm not going to give up on us."

I walk past him and he makes an attempt to grab at my arm. I bat his hand away with force and give him my most threatening face. "Get *OFF* my porch, NOW!"

This is a side that I am sure Steve has never seen of me. I cannot say I ever got mad in front of him, so right now he looks a little bit out of sorts with my outburst.

"I will leave now Sarah, but we are not done here. I will come back when you are not so angry and we will finish this talk. I'm not giving up." He finishes his last sentence to my back because at this point I am already retreating back into the house.

I slam the door behind me and I just snap. I take the card and throw it with all my power, then take my arm and swipe the flower vase off the table, and watch it fall and shatter to the floor. With the sudden crash, I throw my hands to my mouth. Once the rage mellows in my brain, quickly come the tears. I begin to cry. It hits me harder and harder every second I stand in that kitchen staring at the array of roses and broken glass covering the floor. I can't do this. I run out of the kitchen and up to my room. Slamming the door, I throw myself on my bed and cry so hard I think crack a rib.

I must have passed out after my crazy display of waterworks. I sit up to look at the clock, noticing it is pretty late in the day. Jack will be here soon. I go to the bathroom to wash my face and can't hide the fact that my face is puffy and red. Maybe I can lie and tell him I had an allergic reaction.

Yeah, to ex-boyfriends.

I put on more makeup than usual, hoping to hide my blotchy face, then go to pack some things and head downstairs. I start to feel guilty at the mess I abruptly left in the kitchen and go to clean it up. As I enter the kitchen I notice it is all gone. No glass, no flowers. Someone had picked it all up while I was sleeping. Feeling even worse now, knowing it was probably my poor mother, I venture out to find her. The front door is open so I assume she is outside. I open the door to walk outside and see Aunt Raines sitting at the end of the driveway, with a bucket of red roses, and a table. She has a sign in one hand, and a glass, presumably of vermouth, in the other.

I walk down the driveway to get a better look.

"Aunt Raines, what are you doing here?" I ask curiously.

She responds in the world's most chipper voice. "Oh why hello there, sweet baby!"

Just then, a car pulls up and a man gets out. He walks up to what looks like some tables set up with her jewelry. He skims the items, then chooses a set of earrings. He approaches Aunt Raines, hands her some money, and in return she hands him a handful of roses. He thanks her, gets back in his car and drives away.

What the...?

"Take a seat, baby. Don't strain yourself." She points to the lawn chair next to her. As I skeptically sit, she continues. "See now, I found all these roses in the trash and just couldn't let them go to waste. I dug them out and put them in this here bucket. I made some signs for Free Roses and set them all along the main road ahead there. People come and pick some free roses, then look at my pretty jewelry. I have had three buyers so far today!"

I look at her completely stunned.

"I figured these flowers were tainted and came from nothing good, so I wanted to help get rid of them. The vermouth is helping me do it in a kind manner. And it's helping me sell my jewelry!"

Again, another car pulls up, and a lady exits her vehicle. She walks up to the table of jewelry and begins inspecting Aunt Raines' pieces. As I sit here speechless, I watch the woman purchase a ring, take a complimentary batch of roses, and then she is on her way.

Impressive...

I am so overcome with emotion I think I am going to start to cry all over again.

"Thank you," I say to her in a hushed voice, trying not to break.

"Oh no need to thank me, honey. I've watched you bouncing around here the last couple of weeks and I see someone who is getting her life back. It ain't no secret you have love again in that sweet heart of yours." She takes a swig of her vermouth and continues. "I told you before, baby. Sometimes negative life-changing things have to happen for the positive ones to break through."

She was so right.

"I love you, Aunt Raines."

"I love you too, sweet child. "

Just then, a giant truck pulls into the driveway and Jack gets out. He looks at us both suspiciously and walks our way.

"Starting the weekend without me?" he asks; I'm assuming he spots Aunt Raines' half-empty glass.

"Not me. I'm waiting for you. Don't worry," I say and stand up to greet him. I place a soft kiss on his cheek.

"You ready?" he asks.

"Yep. Let me go get my things," I say and go running into the house. Steve hurdle dissolved. I put it in the back of my mind and pack it away under yesterday's trash.

I grab my things and head back out to meet an awaiting Jack. I can tell his curiosity at the vision of Aunt Raines. He says his good-byes and helps me in the truck.

Once en route, he reaches behind his seat and pulls out a bouquet of assorted yellow flowers. He sets them in my lap and continues to focus on driving.

What's with today and flowers?

I pick up the beautiful bouquet of yellow flowers. "What's the special occasion?" I ask.

"You're my special occasion," he replies.

Did I mention that I probably love him?

I don't know where this comes from. Well I do, but I end up blurting it out anyway.

"Why yellow?" I ask like that isn't A) unappreciative, and B) unappreciative.

"Because it's a color that reminds me of you. Vibrant and happy. And it's been both since your car took a nosedive into the back of my truck."

That's it.

Without a single thought about traffic laws, I hurdle myself at him and wrap my arms around his neck.

"*Whoa...*" He screeches as he nearly sideswipes a fire hydrant. "What was that for?"

"It was for being you," I say with the biggest smile on my face. I decline the option to go back to my seat and stay matted up against Jack's frame until we arrive at our destination.

Chapter 31

The drive is pretty quiet but extremely loud at the same time. Neither one of us offers up conversation, but the emotions that are radiating off both of us say enough. The way my body hums when I'm so close to his... I lean my head on his shoulder while he drives. I can hear Jack sigh in contentment. The gesture is so simple but so perfect. We enter in the city and pull up to a restaurant. Jack gets out and allows the valet to take his keys.

"Wait, what are we doing? I thought we were going back to your place?" I say, not even realizing how far we've driven already.

"We are. After I feed you dinner."

Oh-kay.

We walk into the restaurant and from the outside you would not think it was anything fancy. The sign is hidden and I wouldn't have even known it was here if Jack hadn't guided me towards the door.

"—Hey Jack! Good to see you! We have a special table for you. Right this way."

A small plump man about in his 40s with a thick Italian accent greets us and shakes jack's hand. He looks my way and smiles in what seems to be approval.

"Thanks, Antonio."

Jack grabs my hand and I follow him and the man named Antonio to this back room where a table is set for two with multiple candles glowing in the dimmed light.

I look around at how small and homely the place is. There aren't many people in the restaurant but you can tell it probably gets pretty cramped.

An epiphany hits me, but before I can actually bring the thought to my mouth, Jack speaks.

"Starting to look familiar to you?"

"Yes!" I exclaim. "This is the restaurant you are working on!"

"The one *we* are working on. And yes." Jack smiles.

He pulls out the chair for me to sit then walks around to the other chair and seats himself. I continue to look around in astonishment. This place is amazing! The layouts that Jack created would be perfect for this restaurant. The open plan and the see-through kitchen would bring so much more business. It all makes perfect sense now as well with the outside signage. Just putting my design and placing it into the real space here would be glorious.

"You look happy," he says breaking my thoughts.

"I am." And it is the truth. *I am* happy. *I am not* even sure I have ever been this happy. I can't even remember ever truly being happy with Steve. With my job. With living. It just didn't compare to the feelings I am having now.

Jack reaches out and grabs my hand. He brings it to his mouth and presses a gentle kiss to my palm.

"I'm glad..." he says.

Chapter 32

Dinner turns out to be incredible. The food alone is a reason to be a returning customer at this place. I'm sure that even if the place was left as-is, it would still be successful.

Antonio personally brought out each course, and took his time explaining to me the detailed ingredients and cooking methods that go into each dish. I could tell that Jack has been through this all before, since he was not paying as much attention to Antonio as he was paying attention to *me*.

In between courses, Jack explained to Antonio that I had finished the project on his restaurant and was ready to sit down and formulate the final steps. Antonio, of course, was over the moon with excitement and kissed my hands and my cheeks so many times, I lost count.

After a while, Antonio finally disappeared back into the kitchen.

"I am stuffed," I say with a sigh. I am sure I cannot move at this point.

"Antonio spoiled you with all his entrees. He usually doesn't personally feed individual bites to his customers."

At that, I can't help but laugh. Antonio did insist on preparing the perfect bite of lasagna fagioli so I would get all the flavors.

"This place is amazing," I say. "I'm not sure it even needs a revamp with the food and a person like Antonio keeping busy."

"Well then just imagine how well it will do with your touch on it," he says, never taking his eyes off me.

Let's talk about where my touch will hopefully be shortly.

"So, speaking of touch, are you ready to get out of here?" I say in my most whispered seductive voice ever.

"I'm not done yet, babe," he says.

Why would he want to hang out at a restaurant when I just offered him a way better plan? I'm totally baffled...but also, did he just call me *babe*? Because I think my lady parts just did a summersault.

I see Antonio returning from the corner of my eye. I notice he is coming towards us holding a plate with a slice of cake, with a lit candle on top.

Antonio sets the plate in front of me, bows to Jack and then retreats back into the kitchen.

Ohmygod!

"Happy Birthday," Jack says to me in a deep sultry voice.

"How did you—?" *Oh my god! I forgot my own birthday!?* With everything that has been going on lately, I didn't even remember what month it was!

"How did you know?" I manage to ask.

I am so taken aback by the effort once again that Jack is going through to make me happy. This is just too much for me. I do only what I know to do in times when my emotions get the best of me.

I start to cry.

I can feel the tears falling down my cheeks. I see the pained and surprised look on Jack's face, then I grab my face and bury it into my hands.

"What's wrong?" he asks. "Why are you so upset?" He reaches out to try and pull my hands away from my face. I let him and then I look across the table at his worried expression.

"Why are you doing this to me?" I say, unable to further elaborate my question.

"Doing what?" Jack replies with a sense of shock and confusion in his voice.

"Being so perfect and so wonderful. For making me so happy again. For causing me to fall so incredibly, deeply and crazy in love with you." When I finish, I put my face back into my hands. I can hear Jack exhale a breath which he seemed to have been holding throughout my whole tirade.

He moves the candled cake away, reaches across the table and with both hands cups my face. He lifts my face so I have no choice but to make eye contact with him."Because I can't stop being in love with you if I tried. I think I've been in love with you since day one. And all I think about and all I crave is to make you happy, to make you smile, and possibly to hear you scream my name on occasion."

WOW...

I sniffle and wipe the tears that are falling down my face. "I'm sorry Jack, I don't know why I'm crying."

"It's OK," he responds reassuringly.

"I'm in love with you, Jack."

"And I with you, Sarah."

I lean over the table as best I can without setting my shirt on fire and grab his face and crush his mouth to mine. He mirrors the same move and then we're both head-locked in a passionate kiss. This time, the kiss seems different. With more meaning, more emotion. After admitting the strong emotions that were lingering at the tips of both our minds for some time, it all comes out in our kiss. It feels more...*real*. Eventually we both break for air. I pull away and lean back in my chair.

He speaks first. "Now can we finally move on and cross another notch off your list," he says.

"And which one would that be?" I ask.

He picks up the cake with the candle still lit.

"Make a wish, baby."

Chapter 33

Waiting until we got fully into Jack's house was simply not an option. With so many words and feelings being tossed around, there was no way we were going to be able to keep our hands off each other long enough to make it in the house, let alone the bedroom.

After heavily making out in Jack's truck, we finally head towards the house. Jack is carrying me while I have my legs wrapped around his waist and arms around his neck, my tongue deeply down this throat.

I can't believe he told me he loves me. I can't believe I spit out that I love him! Was it too soon? I don't even care. My feelings for him are running so deep that I'm sure I could have told him after day one.

He said he loved me since day one.

The thought just pushes me even deeper down love's throat.

"Turn the knob," he says through his teeth and my lips.

Getting good at not breaking our kiss, I continue to wrap my tongue around his while I take an arm away from his neck and push my arm behind me to open the door, which crashes open and we stumble inside.

Jack walks in and stops just long enough to kick the door closed with his foot.

"I love the way you kiss me," he rumbles. "I can sense your desire through your giving mouth." He walks me back towards the bedroom. I am getting familiar with this routine.

This time, instead of tossing me on the bed he gently sets me down on my two feet. We lock eyes and I can't help but notice our breathing is heavy and Jack is straining to keep himself in control.

This time I feel like it's my turn offer the dessert. I slide down to my knees and start unbuckling his jeans. Pulling his jeans down, along with his boxers, I can see his arousal in great force. Jack is definitely ready for dessert.

I look at him one final time then place my mouth around home plate. He groans so loudly I almost pull away. The inkling of hesitation sends his hand in my hair and then he cradles my head to continue.

"Oh my god you feel so good around me," he groans in a strangled voice.

I continue my feast of pleasuring him while I add a bonus feature and cup his goods. That receives another groan and a squeeze of my hair.

I can feel how bad this is affecting him with the hardness of him in my mouth. Every movement I offer, he clenches his hand in my hair tighter and the sounds of approval are beyond satisfying. Before I know it, he yanks up and aggressively tosses me on the bed. He throws off his shirt and flings it on the floor.

Jack crawls onto the bed and leans just above me. He unbuttons my jeans and yanks them down my legs. Then he disassembles me from my panties. Moving on top of me, he lifts my shirt from my stomach and over my head. He then proceeds to toss my jeans, shirt, and panties into the growing mound of clothes on the floor.

"You are so beautiful, Sarah," he practically hisses, then he dips down to press his lips to my chest. He moves alongside my breasts while taking one hand behind my back and unclasping my bra. With ease, he breaks me away from my bra. "Simply beautiful," he says again, then presses his open mouth around my nipple.

God he feels so good. I arch my back to give him fuller access and he eagerly obliges, cupping my breast in his hands while erotically assaulting my nipple with his mouth. I may climax if he keeps this up. I am about to beg him to do dirty things to me if he doesn't give me what my body is so desperately aching for.

Knowing my body well by now, Jack releases my breast and nudges my legs open with his hand. With one hard push, he thrusts himself inside me.

I am seeing stars...and I haven't even climaxed yet! This is how amazing Jack is. His left hand is gripping my hip so tightly it is burning my skin, while his right hand is cupping my breast.

He does what I am hoping at that point and goes for the take. His mouth wraps around my nipple and I moan so loudly I don't even recognize my own voice. I am so close to exploding but I don't want this to end. We are wrapped up tightly in each other and it feels so good.

I can tell Jack is at the brink of breaking because his thrusts are gradually speeding up and they are getting harder. Deeper. I wrap my legs around his waist to remove any extra space between us and hold on. Two more pounding thrusts and we both simultaneously climax.

I feel his body crush into mine as he tries to control his breathing. His weight is heavy but feels both wonderful and safe. I hold him in place, hoping he will stay this way forever.

I can feel our hearts starting to beat in unison at a normal pace. And then Jack lifts his head and kisses my neck.

"I love kissing you, Sarah. Your skin is so soft," he says, his breath slowly steadying. "I love hearing you come. Your sweet moans drive me insane."

I take my hand and brush away the loose hair hanging in his face. "You are the perfect one, Jack," I tell him.

We stare at each other for some time until he breaks the silence.

"God I love you," he says, brushing his nose along mine.

"Well I love God too. But I think I may love you more."

Jack chuckles, then grabs a hold of my hips in preparation for round two.

Chapter 34

I wake up to Jack nuzzling my goods. Best wake up call for me—ever. Breakfast of Champions for him. After wearing ourselves out...twice...we take a shower. It is truly amazing the things one finds enough space to do in one's shower, I have to admit.

Because it's Sunday, I am so exhausted. In the past 48 hours—which consisted of Friday night on repeat into Saturday, then of course into Sunday—I am unsure my body can hold up for another orgasm. Not that I am one to wave the white flag but if I don't get a decent amount of food and caffeine in me, I am going to die of sexual exhaustion. What would my poor mother say? Would they write *death by sexual exhaustion* on my tombstone?

Freshly clean, dressed in jeans and one of Jack's T-shirts, I head towards the kitchen, where Jack is already preparing breakfast. Or lunch. I am not even sure what time it is. I enter the kitchen to the punch of coffee and various other aromas invading my senses.

"Oh good heavens, that smells glorious!" I exclaim. "I am starving."

After Jack pulls some sort of egg concoction out of the oven, he sets down a plate and slides a variety of Danishes and fruit in front of me.

"Did you sleep well?" he asks, while pulling bacon off the stove.

"When? I don't remember doing any sleeping." When he turns to me, I look at him and continue. "I'm not sure anyone sleeps when inside this house. I might have to go on a sabbatical from you just to get some sleep!"

Jack starts to laugh and slides two slices of bacon on my plate. He reaches over and pours coffee into the mug in front of me and places the cream and sugar within my reach.

"If you dare try and hide from me, I will have to find you, and definitely go back on my word and tie you up in my bedroom and share you with no one."

I debate whether or not to argue with him but just looking at him makes me realize that there might be a hint of truth to his statement. OK, note to self: no hiding from Jack or he will come find me.

He finishes making another plate, then sits down beside me on the island bar. He grabs for a piece of Danish and fruit and turns to me.

"Open," he says and slowly begins to feed me.

We spend the next hour eating breakfast, half of which Jack insists on feeding me himself. I ask how he became such a good cook, and he admits that he learned the history of fancy food from his ex who was a food connoisseur for a high-profile food magazine in Chicago. So the second-hand food lessons came with the territory. I have to admit, it gives me a bitter taste in my mouth. As much as I enjoy a good piece of creamy Danish and eggs, I do not enjoy knowing how someone could just get up and leave a man who just lost his only family. Why couldn't she just ditch her *so-called future plans*? But then that thought makes me realize: God, I think I would do anything for Jack.

I also don't want to picture Jack sitting in his kitchen with his ex, feeding each other fancy foods, while laughing. Having his mouth on someone else sends shocks of jealousy through my brain and body. Pushing the jealousy aside, I continue to let him press an assortment of delicious food into my mouth. I can tell he is watching my facial expressions after each pairing, waiting to see the satisfaction of my taste buds as it plays on my face.

"I'm going to take you home shortly, don't worry," he tells me. "You can get some sleep then. I have a small crew finishing up your parents' addition by the end of the week and need to do a final walk-through to make sure everything is in place."

"So you don't have any plans for me today?" I ask. I partially say it as a joke since the past week he has possessively planned our days, but partially because I am kind of disappointed that we are going to be separating.

"Don't worry, my love. I have a whole set of plans for you. But they require you to recoup. And I'm not only talking about catching up on sleep."

My lady parts take a leap and spin.

Jack clears his plate, then rises to put the cooking pans in the sink. Apparently he needed a food boost more than I did.

"I see. Well then, do what you must. I have some things I need to take care of, besides sleeping anyway. I just left poor Aunt Raines and her vermouth to fend for themselves on Friday. It probably will do me some good to spend time mending any damage I've caused."

Jack laughs and clears the counter, then he walks around the island. "Well, good," he says. "So now that we have our days planned out we can move on to planning our night."

He gives me a devilish grin. I have to look away because it is almost too intense to keep eye contact.

Jack stands there and watches me finish the food on my plate. Once I am done, he takes my empty dish and places it in the sink next to his.

He turns to walk towards me, then he makes his way around the kitchen bar to my stool. He spreads my legs so he can stand in between them and brings his hands to my head, his fingers through my wet hair.

"I love you," he says without doubt or hesitation in his voice. "I know this is very soon to admit such strong feelings, but it doesn't matter to me. I can't change how I feel."

I simply melt in his hands. I turn to press my cheek into his palm.

"I love you too, Jack."

This is what fairy tales are made of. I know it, I know it, I know it...

Chapter 35

On cloud nine, we drive back to my parents' house. Not making too much conversation during the drive, I think about my future. What it all means. I feel like it's about time I leave the nest, *again*, and get a place for myself. I seem to have taken up residency at Jack's, but it will probably be too soon to drop off my toothbrush there. I know we both spilled the love beans to each other, but that doesn't mean he wants to move in with me. I mean, even after seven years with Steve and *practically* living in each other's apartments, we never even made that leap.

Jack breaks my thoughts. "How long do you plan on staying with your parents?"

Wow, is this guy in my head or what!?

"I'm not sure," I tell him as casually as I can muster. "I guess I never really had to stay there to begin with. To be honest I have a nice little nest egg that I'm sitting on. I made a good amount at Hamilton Corp and never really had a reason to spend any of it. I barely paid rent because Stacey's parents took over the living expenses, no questions asked."

"So why did you choose to go home if you could have just gotten your own place?" he asks.

"I don't know. I think at that time I needed home. I needed comfort in something, or someone. No matter what I was going through, I knew my parents would give that to me. And honestly, at that point I was so messed up it was just safer that way."

"Well the only thing that is messed up now is your hair after what you made me do to you after breakfast," he says, trying suddenly to defuse the topic.

I slap him on the shoulder because I know he is messing with me. Then I count to three to not make it obvious and look in the mirror at my hair. Because seriously, what he did to me after breakfast really did mess up my hair...

Chapter 36

We make it to my parents' house and luckily do not find Aunt Raines still in the driveway selling her jewelry and discarding roses to strangers.

We enter the house to find my mother in the kitchen cutting out coupons.

"Oh, hello dear. How are you? Oh goodness, what happened to your hair?"

I am going to kill Jack.

"Nothing, Mom. I drove with the windows down," I reply, trying to ignore Jack's snort behind me.

"Hello Jack, I'm glad you're here. A worker of yours was asking me some questions about the deck area and I wasn't sure how to answer him. Maybe you can speak with him for me?"

Just then the doorbell rings.

"I'll get that," I say to Jack. "You go help my mom."

"All right..." he says and escorts my mother out the back door.

I pretty much hop to the front door humming. Love will do that to a person. I open the door to greet our guest, and find Steve standing on my front step.

I freeze.

What the...?

Apparently Steve has been staring at the street waiting for the door to open. He turns to see me standing in the doorway.

"Hello, Sar," he says, his voice soft.

My face must be bright red, I am so furious! "I thought I made myself clear the other day when I said you were to get lost and not come back!" I spit out.

Steve flinches like I physically struck him.

This is not happening to me right now. He is supposed to be gone and out of my life. I have Jack, the amazing Jack in my backyard, and Steve is on my front porch. I don't know whether to laugh, cry, or pass out.

"You should not have come back," I say coldly.

"I wouldn't have come if you would have accepted my apology the first time and come home with me."

I am getting a bit panicky at this point. I really do not want to have Steve run into Jack and the tension that would ensue. I step outside the house and shut the door.

"Now is not a good time, Steve. You need to leave."

"But I need to talk to you, Sarah," he insists. "I need you to understand."

"*Understand*?" I say, raising my voice even louder this time. "I'm not sure that catching you fucking my best friend...well, *ex* best friend...leaves anything to be understood. I understand perfectly!"

OK, yeah, now I'm pissed.

"We left it as if you were going to take some time to think about things. I told you we weren't done, Sarah. I know you needed time. And I have given it to you. I am here now to take you home."

"Are you insane, Steve? Really, are you *actually* insane?! I am not going anywhere with you. What part of *you got caught cheating so we are over* do you not understand?!"

"Sarah, this is about us. I know you felt something when we were together the other day. It meant something. That kiss meant something."

Ugh. The only thing I can remember about that kiss is how I wanted to sear my lips off after he made that attempt.

"You wanted me," he continues. "You remember how good we were. Don't do this. We can be good again." He keeps begging, and all I can think is how I want to run to Jack and have him make me forget by touching me all over my body with his lips and mouth.

Jack.

"Sarah…" he says, putting his hand on my shoulder. "That's not what I meant. I know you want us to get back together. Please give me a moment—"

Out of nowhere I hear the front door slam shut. I turn to see Jack standing behind me with a look of death on his face.

Oh god! How long has he been there? What did he hear?

He sees Steve's hand on my shoulder and instantly his jaw sets into a rock solid clench. I am not sure at this point if I should guard Steve because Jack might kill him, or if I should just step in front of Jack because, well, because Jack still might kill him.

"Is everything OK out here?" Jack asks.

"Everything is fine," I manage to say somewhat calmly. "This guy was just leaving."

"This guy!?" Steve exclaims. "That's what I am now?! Some guy? Steve spits out his words almost on a whine.

Here we go.

OK, now I think Jack is definitely considering killing Steve. Not that I want to take a second out of my life to speak to Steve, but at this point, I can tell that Jack's patience is running real thin and I need to get Steve out of here.

So I do the only thing I can think of make that happen.

"Listen, Steve. I will talk to you, but not now OK? Just please, leave. Give me some time."

"How much time, Sarbear? I need you." OK, now he's done it.

I feel Jack take my shoulders and push me out of the way. This is so not going to end well.

"I think it's time for you to leave, buddy," Jack says with his last ounce of self-control.

"Leave? Who are you?" Steve turns to me and belts out, "Sarah, who is this guy?"

Steve totally catches me off guard. I don't know how to answer that question. What is Jack to me? We said 'I love you' to each other, but we never talked about dating or girlfriend/boyfriend status. Are we exclusive? I just don't know what to say, so I say, well, probably the worst thing I can possibly say in this moment.

"He's a friend, OK? Now please just leave."

I feel Jack tense up beside me. I don't have to look at him to see the shock and betrayal in his eyes.

"OK, but if I don't hear from you I'm coming back. We will talk, Sarbear," Steve finishes. He tries to reach for me, but Jack stands in his way. Not wanting to go to battle with him, Steve decides it is best to skip the embrace and he turns and walks to his fancy BMW and drives away.

I just stand there.

Afraid.

Jack speaks first.

"How many times have you seen him since we've been together?" he asks, his voice chilling.

"Once before today," I answer.

"Were you ever going to tell me about your little make-out session with your ex?" he asks, his voice searing.

"Yes, I was going to... Maybe. I don't know. It happened so fast. It wasn't what I was expecting. I didn't know he was going to kiss me." I am stuttering over all my words. I just don't know how this got so—

"So I can assume that day I came to pick you up, those flowers, they were from Romeo?"

"Yes," I answer on a scared whisper. I don't like where this is going. Jack is sweltering anger and I can feel it coming off his skin. He won't even look at me.

"When he was sticking his tongue down your throat I assume you didn't bother mentioning me?"

"It wasn't like that, Jack," I say in almost panic. I can tell this is not going to end well. I turn to face him, but he is like stone, staring out into the lawn. It is obvious he can't even look at me.

"He said you two were together. Did you fuck him?" he spits out.

"God, no! It wasn't like that!"

"So just now you let him put his hands on you and called you, what? Your bedroom pet name he has for you?!" His tone is harsh and striking.

"No! Jack, it's not like that. I just wanted him gone. I didn't know any other way—"

"So you degrade me, when I am trying to defend you from this jerk who tossed you aside for your fucking roommate, so you can just refer to me as nothing more than your friend?!" Now he is yelling.

I have pure panic in my tone and fear on my face. He is so angry. I should have told him about Steve coming over. I should have told him everything, but I just wanted to forget. I didn't want it to be significant enough to even talk about.

"Jack, please, listen to me," I plead and attempt to pull his shoulders to look at me. Shocking me, he throws my hands off him.

"You know Sarah, I really thought you were better than that. I thought you were smarter and realized you deserved better. I guess I thought I had a part in that. But you seem to be still too swept up in your ex to see what's around you," he says flatly.

"What!? What are you talking about? I *do* see what's in front of me. Jack, it's you I see. I love you!" I say in sheer panic. What is happening right now?

"Listen Sarah, I hope you are happy. If it's not with me I hope it's not back with him. But I'm not going to sit here and watch you fuck around with me while you debate whether you want to go back to that." As he finishes, he points in the directions of Steve's long-gone vehicle.

I try to grab at him again, and again he brushes me away from him. He starts walking away from me, toward his truck.

"Jack! Wait! What are you doing!? You can't just leave!" I start to cry because I don't know what else to do. God, he can't be leaving me right now!

"Jack, please let me explain," I beg on a strangled cry.

"You had all weekend to explain. I'm done," he says and leaves me to stare at his back. He jumps in his truck and peels out of the driveway. He sends the truck in gear and takes off.

I drop to my knees.

What did I just do?

I begin to cry uncontrollably.

I cannot say that I have ever felt such pain before. I didn't feel this pain walking into my apartment and catching Stacey and Steve together, or after the outburst at Hamilton Corp and consequently losing my job. I didn't feel this much pain when I came crawling home and locked myself in my bedroom for three months. What have I done?

I have ruined it. Everything. Why did I feel I had to guard Steve's feelings about who Jack was? Why did I say what I said? I knew exactly what he was to me. He was my heart. The one I loved more than the air I breathed. I shouldn't have guarded that from Steve, because I felt nothing for Steve. Now, for the first time, I realize that there was nothing there for him in me. There wasn't even hurt or hatred. Jack took that all away. I found peace with Jack. And now he was gone.

I continue to cry because I just don't know how to get myself in order or get my emotions on track. Where do I go from here? I feel sick to my stomach. I can't seem to catch my breath and so I start to hyperventilate. Keeping up my choking sobs at this point is completely useless. I believe this is what being completely broken feels like. He is gone and now I have nothing.

I sit in the lawn and just bawl. At some point I remember someone picking me up and carrying me into the house. I assume it was my poor dad. I cry in bed while listening to my mother sooth me with kind words while patting my back. I remember Aunt Raines coming in and out, trying to get me to drink some vermouth. I continue to lie in my bed in hopes that this was all a bad dream. I can't be going through this again. And especially not with Jack.

I let sleep finally take me, hoping I will wake up from this nightmare. I squeeze my eyes shut and eventually my world goes black.

Chapter 37

Two days pass since Jack left. I try calling him at work and on his cell, but I just get his voicemail. In the beginning I left messages pleading for him to call me back, with no response. When I got up the nerve to just face him, I drove to his site to catch him at work, but Bill told me he had taken a job out of town and wouldn't be back for a few more days. Without looking pathetic and desperate I thanked him and went on my way. I just couldn't understand what went so wrong so fast. I couldn't wrap my head around it. He wouldn't even let me explain. It was killing me to not be able tell him how I really felt.

Two more days come and go and still no word from Jack. I had resorted to spending more time with Aunt Raines which only turned ugly after my excessive vermouth binge. It was like clockwork after my 5th glass: I would call Jack's phone and leave crying, sobbing, blubbering drunken messages. Not that I made any sense in them. Aunt Raines eventually unplugged the phone on me during happy hour just to save me some dignity.

I am so unhappy it hurts. The last thing Jack said to me before he stormed away was he hoped if it wasn't with him at least I found happiness. It kills me that he thinks my happiness isn't with him. He is all I want—all I ever wanted. I am sick not to see his face, feel his touch, the scent of his skin, his breath; it's like an addiction I am being forced to wean off of.

I hate myself.

I hate myself for being so stupid.

Two days after the blowout, Steve called to try and talk, and I just went crazy. I screamed at the top of my lungs how I was never going to take a second of my time to speak to him about anything. How we were so through, and the man that had been standing next to me was the man that I was madly in love with. I ended it by telling him to go hell, never contact me again. Three days later, a courier service dropped off five boxes of my stuff. Apparently Steve got the message.

Which brings me pretty much to today. My day is going to consist of bonding with vermouth and Aunt Raines. She luckily volunteered to participate in my 'Get it the fuck off my property' garage sale, which consists of all the boxes Steve sent over. We've posted Garage Sale signs down the block and of course added 'free stuff'. It takes two glasses of vermouth each for Aunt Raines and I to drag all the boxes to the front lawn. Box by box we dump the contents in the lawn. We set up our chairs in the middle of the lawn, a mini foldout table to hold the bottle and shaker, and sit in anticipation.

I am on my fourth glass when I see a truck driving down our street. My heart takes a leap hoping that it is Jack. The truck stops on the curb and parks. Holding my breath, I watch, but I'm disappointed when I see Bill get out of the truck.

He walks our way, with a bit of curiosity.

"What's going on here?" he asks suspiciously.

"We are having a garage sale. Everything is free," I slur. *Man, how many have I had so far?*

"I see that," he says, eyeing me with sympathy. "I'm sorry to bother you Sarah, I know you probably thought it was Jack. He sent me over here to sign off on the addition project. Since the guys are done and all."

He doesn't even want to see me. I know Jack has to sign off on everything, but I am that bad in his eyes. Without even realizing I am doing it, I swat a tear that escapes my eye.

"I'm sorry, Sarah. He's really upset right now. Give him some time."

I just nod. I try to hide the hurt and pain that is seeping from my face but can't. The tears keep falling. One would think that at some point they would stop.

"He loves you, Sarah. I can see it. He's hurting too right now."

No, it's OK Bill, you don't have to. I understand. Thanks for coming by. My mother is most likely in the kitchen so please see yourself inside," I say and turn to hide my crumbled expression.

"Hey. Listen. It's none of my business, but he gets home tomorrow. I am supposed to meet him at his house at seven in the evening to drop off all of his paperwork. I'm sure you can catch him there."

I turn back and look at Bill. "Thanks," I say quietly.

"No problem," he says. "Good luck with the garage sale." He smiles sympathetically and walks into the house.

I have so many thoughts running through my head. Do I go and force Jack to talk to me? What if he tells me he is done with me? Wait. He's already told me that. I slump back into my chair next to Aunt Raines. How have I made such a mess of my life? Before, it was out of control, sure. But this time it is all my fault. I have brought this pain on myself.

"You OK, sweet girl?" Aunt Raines breaks my thought.

"I don't think so, Aunt Raines. What do I do? Where do I go from here?"

"You go talk to that boy, sweet baby. You tell him how you feel. Make him listen. He will understand what happened."

"I'm not so sure," I say.

"Have some faith in him, baby. He loves you. He will listen."

"And if he doesn't?" I ask with panic again in my stomach, just thinking about him turning me away and that being it.

"Well then at least you tried. You can't say you didn't fight for him."

She is so right. I have to fight. I am just so overwhelmed with uncertainty that he will turn his back to me, and then I will be alone. Without him. I never felt this with Steve. I wasn't so hurt and pained because I wasn't with him anymore; it was merely what he did to me. This time it's different. The loss of Jack near me on a constant basis is suffocating. Without him I feel like I am honestly struggling to breathe.

"Well if he turns me down, I always have you, Aunt Raines," I say, trying to lighten the mood.

"Not for long, sweet child. I'm off to go back home tomorrow, you know that."

Oh my god! Why don't I ever pay attention to dates?! Not only did Jack leave me, and will probably tell me to stay gone, now Aunt Raines is going back home too and I will officially be alone. I'm not sure I can justify vermouth hour on my own.

"I don't want you to go, Aunt Raines," I say, with more emotion in my voice. Everyone is leaving me.

"You will make it just fine, baby. If things get too tight for you around here, my door is always open and you are welcome. The sun is shining every day there. And I can always use some of your beautiful persuasion in my pursuit to sell my jewelry."

I have to laugh at that one. If all else fails I know that I'll always have a place in my Aunt Raines world, with vermouth and big balky jewelry as my life plan. At least life isn't totally hopeless.

"Thanks, Aunt Raines. I will make sure to keep that as a last resort."

She grabs my hand and squeezes.

The rest of the day is less eventful. At some point both Aunt Raines and I pass out in our chairs. Right before though, some nice lady came by and was so overtaken by all the free stuff that she pretty much cleaned us out, mumbling things about fancy silk and brand names, until she couldn't fit anything else in her car. She even took the picture of Steve that I had in a frame. I was happy to part with it. She was so overwhelmed that she might have even been crying. Well that made two of us. That's about when things get fuzzy. I wasn't sure when Bill left, and was a bit embarrassed at my possible unconscious state when he did. I was hoping he had kept it to himself and not mentioned anything to Jack about my over indulging shenanigans.

I wake up as the sun is setting. I nudge Aunt Raines to signal her inside and then go upstairs to my room. I change out of my clothes and pull on one of Jack's big T-shirts over my head. I lie down in the bed and try to decide what I should do next. I love him. I know that more than I know anything else right now. If I don't at least try and make him understand then I can only blame myself. Bill said that Jack was hurting, and that thought tears me apart. He did nothing to deserve this from me and I've hurt him. With that thought, I settle more into my pillow and hug Jack's shirt.

Working myself into a frenzy about what tomorrow could be, I finally start to drift. I'm assuming the five glasses of vermouth have a part in that. Then, thankfully, I sleep.

Chapter 38

The day is dragging at a snail's pace. As it works, everything seems to go slower when you're waiting for something. Deadlines would come before you know. Times like when your love life hangs from the rafters. I can swear the clock is ticking backwards for most of today. I sit on the newly finished back deck addition with my mother who has been pretty quiet all day. It is new to be sober at this time of the day, but then again, I probably shouldn't start drinking since I have to drive, not to mention sell my life and heart to a man.

I think about showering at this point but it takes effort I really don't have. My stomach is in such a knot and I'm not sure I should be driving a vehicle. The chances of me hitting a tree on my way over are pretty high.

"You ready, sweet baby?" Aunt Raines says, interrupting my thoughts.

Oh god. It's already time? I have to drop her off at the airport and then I will go to Jack's. Bill said that he is expected there by seven. That will leave me some time to pace his front lawn and decide whether I should abort the mission and run like the wind.

"I am, Aunt Raines," I say sullenly. I am going to miss Aunt Raines. She has been such a rock for me these past few weeks. She stood by me in my times of sadness and helped me off my ledge of misery. "I'm not ready to see you go, Aunt Raines," I say, my eyes filling up with tears.

"Oh baby, you'll be OK. You are a strong woman. He will understand, baby. Have faith," she says. She comes up to me and embraces me in a big warm hug.

"I hope so, Aunt Raines," I say. "I hope so."

Chapter 39

I drop Aunt Raines off at the airport and cry out my good-byes. She makes me promise that I will come visit her soon, and then I'm on my way.

As I drive to Jack's I deeply regret not bringing a plastic bag, because I am pretty close to barfing in my lap. My nerves are so out of control I'm starting to get scared. This has to go OK. He has to listen to me. He just has to.

I pull into his long driveway and see that his truck is not here. I'm thankful for that. It gives me some time to gather my emotions and get my thoughts in order.

I get out of the car and walk up to his front porch step and take a seat. I'm trying to figure out what I say first... Do I beg? Do I just start spitting out 'I'm sorry' and 'please take me back or I'll die'? What if he doesn't even want me anymore? Then I take a look at myself and what I'm wearing. I haven't showered in god-knows-how-long and my hair is in a sloppy makeshift ponytail. To the average person I may look homeless.

Oh god.

Why didn't I shower!? I'm about to get up and take off because this is a bad idea and maybe once I've cleaned myself up and made a list, or a speech, I should come back.

Just then I hear the sounds of Jack's truck pulling up to the house.

I sit back down. "Calm down... Calm Down," I repeat to myself over and over. I don't think that is possible but if I don't, I'm not going to even have to talk to Jack because I will have keeled over of a heart attack right on his front step.

Imagine having to dump your ex-lover's body somewhere after already thinking you told them to get lost...*uggghhhh...*

I notice that Jack sees my presence and hesitates to get out. That can't be a good sign.

In time he jumps out, with determination, and walks by me. "What are you doing here?" he says, so harsh and cold.

He doesn't even stop. He takes his steps two at a time, and walks past me.

"I want to talk," I say in a rushed voice. "I need to talk to you." He doesn't seem to be giving me any stage time, and I'm pretty sure in about two seconds his door is going to slam in my face.

"I'm not sure there is anything to talk about, Sarah. You shouldn't have come here."

Oh god, this is so not going well. Jack gets the front door open and walks into his house. I frantically follow.

"Jack, I need you to listen. I need you to understand. I love you!"

Oh that was the wrong thing to say. He turns so quickly and ends up in my face. I almost trip backwards.

"Don't you say that to me!" he yells straight into my face.

"Jack, but I do, I need you to just—"

"Just what, Sarah? Listen to you explain how while you and I were in bed together, you were making up with your ex-boyfriend?!" he hisses in my face.

I try to grab for him, but he throws my arms off him and turns around to walk towards his kitchen.

"Jack, it wasn't like that. It's not like that. I wasn't making up with him. He grabbed me and kissed me. It caught me off guard. I pulled away. He took it the wrong way. I told him to leave immediately after!"

Now I was spitting out my story. He hadn't been giving me any room for explanation before, and the way he had started spinning it, it sounded horrible!

"And you just failed to mention him too?! You failed to mention that while I was pouring my heart out to you, that you had Mr. Rich and Perfect at your front door trying make things better? *Kissing you*?!"

"Jack, it wasn't like that!" I say in a desperate cry.

He isn't even listening to me. I start to cry, no shocker there. He won't even turn around to face me. He is leaning into the kitchen island bar with his arm tightly set on the counter and his head dipped down.

"I'm not doing this with you, Sarah," he says almost on a resolve. Like he's already made up his mind.

And it completely breaks me.

I let out a desperate cry and drop to my knees.

"I'm sorry! I'm so sorry, Jack! I love you." I begin to cry harder with nothing else left.

"I love you," I continue, pulling myself together and speaking more calmly. He won't look at me yet, but my eyes bore into him. "It's all I have ever been sure of. I knew the second Steve put his lips on mine that it was never him. I didn't feel anything but closure. I wasn't mad anymore about what had happened because it had turned out to be the best thing someone had ever done to me. Because it brought me to you. I didn't tell you because I didn't want Steve to affect me anymore, let alone to affect you, or *us*. I had made the decision that day that I was moving forward. With you. Then you showed up and just seeing you confirmed it. I knew I was so in love with you that everything was going to be OK. I couldn't have him spoil a single second more of my life. You have to believe me."

And just like that, my emotions come loose again. My sobs are thick and I'm not sure he is even hearing me over them, but I go on.

"It's all that I can hear. The sound of my heart falling deeper and deeper for you. I'm sorry I messed up but I don't know how to fix it."

I feel so defeated. I just don't want to hurt anymore. I put my face in my hands and allow myself to sob uncontrollably.

I hear Jack's footsteps come closer to me, then his whole presence, as he kneels in front of me. He takes my hands in his and pulls them away from my face.

"Shhhhh…" he says, taking my chin in his hand. He lifts my head to make eye contact with him. "Sarah, look at me."

I pick up my head and focus on his beautiful features. He lifts his hand to my face to wipe the tears streaming from my eyes.

"Sarah, calm down. It's OK. I'm sorry. Calm down."

He presses his lips to mine and softly kisses me. Then he pulls away.

"I was so upset. I shouldn't have just left you like that. You deserved to explain. I was so angry at the thought of him touching you and tasting those lips that were mine. I couldn't take it."

I dip my head down again. He wipes more of the tears spilling down my face.

"Sarah, baby, calm down and look at me."

I try to focus on his face but my tears just blur my vision.

"I love you," he says. "I've never been so damn in love with anybody in my entire life. Being without you has been hell for me. To be honest the second I finished some business with Bill, I was going to come and get you. I didn't care anymore what happened. I just needed you. I've missed your touch."

He lets my hands fall to my lap and then he takes his hands and puts them back on each side of my face.

"I missed your sweet taste," he continues while brushing his lips to mine. He pulls away and looks back into my eyes. "I want every part of you here, with me. And since you're here, you saved me the trip of coming after you and kidnapping you."

He then, with power, puts his mouth on mine. I accept him with force and crush my lips to his. I hook my arms around his neck. I think I am crushing his breathing passage but he doesn't seem to be fazed by it.

He quickly stands up, wraps his arms around my waist and picks me up.

"God, I've missed you," he says, his voice hoarse. He maneuvers my legs so they wrap around his waist.

I am finally able to speak again. "I love you, I love you I love you," I repeat over and over as I kiss his lips.

"I love you too, baby," he whispers into my mouth.

Then he walks back towards his bedroom because I'm certain he has makeup sex on his mind. Or maybe that's just me. He enters into the bedroom and moves past the bed, into the bathroom.

Puzzled at his intentions, I pull my head away and look at him in confusion.

"Sarah, who bathes you while I'm not around?" he asks.

"Um... I'm not sure anyone does," I state quite truthfully.

"You smell like vermouth and dirty socks," he says while turning on the shower.

"Showers haven't been the same alone since I've met you."

"I completely agree. So we are going to shower and I'm going to clean you up," he says. "And then I'm going to get you all dirty again."

God I love this man.

He puts me down and starts to pull my shirt over my head. I let him.

He removes my pants. I let him.

Then begins taking his clothes off. *Oh, do I let him.*

As we enter the shower, he kisses my shoulders. He takes both of my hands and places them on the shower's smooth tile wall. I can feel him pressing into me from behind and I am definitely realizing that we might just get a little bit dirtier before we get clean.

Epilogue

Have you ever woken up one day and realized that life was exactly where it's supposed to be? It didn't have to consist of fancy things or big Job titles. Life is truly what you make of it. And that's what makes life perfect. That's what makes it the full package.

It's been five months since our first and only fight. Not that fighting ends up being a bad thing if makeup sex like we had follows it. Since then, Jack so kindly hired me on full-time at Calloway Construction. I spend half my days in Jack's office so he can take private breaks during his meetings and better direct me on my work. And I spend the other half of my days at home, because Jack gives me the time off, along with himself. We don't leave the bedroom much.

I have moved most of my stuff into his place. He asked me to move in shortly after our fight. He reminded me that he had officially kidnapped me and spending any more time apart was not healthy for us. He was right. We spend some of our nights lying in bed giggling with each other while making up bucket lists for ourselves.

Since my permanent job placement at Calloway Construction, word got out that I was now an employee and business was overflowing with small companies and projects that not only insist on Jack's expertise but in my marketing expertise as well. Every time I complete a project, Jack gives me a raise.

We attended the opening of the city communal park and it turned out even more amazing than on paper. There were kids everywhere with happy parents. There are no words to describe the joy I saw on so many faces. It truly made me feel complete with my work.

The restaurant is well on its way to being done with the revamp. Local news did a story on it and once the community got a hold of the news that Calloway Construction was heading the revamp, the curiosity spread like wildfire. Antonio has been booked solid with reservations for months.

I never heard from Steve again. Or Stacey, for that matter. I did get to run into Becky one day at the Starbucks, again, and was notified that they broke it off shortly after I found out, and that Stacey was no longer even in town. I think Becky slipped when she told me about Steve's continuous promiscuous mishaps on company time and how his father and the board members were trying to quietly remove him from the board.

I was unfazed though. It wasn't in me to care. I wished Becky well hoping I seriously did not make a habit of running into her again and again.

I was happy. I was able to climb out of my rut, with the help of a wonderful man. And he took care of me. He loved me for who I was and didn't hesitate to show me every chance he got.

Which brings me to now. I would love to sit here and continue bragging about how good I have it, but I am running late to meet Jack for a sizing at the jeweler. See, he put a ring on my finger two days ago and I said yes.

My name is Sarah Sullivan and this happily ever after is called my life.

The End

Acknowledgements

Thanks to my husband for being my biggest supporter. For all those times you played mommy and daddy which allowed me the time to spread my creative wings. To Michelle, my editor, for holding my hand through this entire journey. Lastly, to all my romance book buddies. Life is just a little bit juicier when you add a pinch of smut to it. This one's for you!

Proof

Made in the USA
Charleston, SC
28 April 2014